IT'S NOT THE HOOKUP, IT'S THE CHASE

ELLE WRIGHT

elle wright

It's Not the Hookup, It's the Chase
Copyright @ 2022 by Elle Wright
Paperback ISBN: 979-8-9854542-1-5

Excerpt from *It's Not Them, It's Only Her*
copyright @ 2023 by Elle Wright

Elle Wrights Books, LLC
Ypsilanti, Michigan
www.ElleWright.com

Copy Editor/Proofreading:
Paulette Nunlee
5-Star Proofing

Cover Design:
Sherelle Green

It's Not the Hookup, It's the Chase

A long time ago, I helped her. Little tips about what to wear, how to leave a man wanting more, ways to be sexy without being too obvious. The guy she'd wanted was wrong for her, though. Still, she'd wanted him anyway and ended up with a broken heart. But she wasn't the only one, because even after I'd made my own intentions known, she walked away.

Now, she's back in town. Still beautiful, still intelligent, still funny, and ready to start over after a bad breakup from someone who never deserved her in the first place.

Want to know when I fell for one of my best friends? I can't even tell you. Somewhere between eating Superman ice cream in her mom's backyard and punching the first boy to ever make her cry.

Want to know how I got friend-zoned? She'd have to tell you. My services—Wingman for Hire—help women drive the men they want crazy. Yet, I couldn't seem to get her to notice me that way.

Want to know what I decided to do about it? The absolute right thing at the wrong time.

Now, everything is different. The past is supposed to be forgotten; the rejection *should* be in the rear-view mirror. And I'm not asking for much… just forever.

Dear Reader

Oh Dex!

This guy has taken up residence in my thoughts for so long. The more he revealed himself, the more I wanted to know. As I wrote his story, I found myself engrossed in him, in his journey. He is everything!

And Charlye…

Transparent Moment. I struggled with my own self-esteem for so many years, falling in love with people I knew couldn't love me the way I deserved. Until I found the one who did. Even then, it seemed unreal because I couldn't bring myself to believe we were destined to live our happily ever after together. Now, twenty+ years later, I wanted to go back to that unsure feeling I had back then. And Charlye came to life. She was such a challenge, because she was so familiar. She was me. And I loved writing her, I loved revisiting feelings that I'd had myself so many years ago.

Just so you know… if you've read Ten Christmas Shots, I wrote about Dallas' very pregnant belly. Well… she wasn't *that* pregnant in the story because it takes place right around the time this novel begins. You'll see how I addressed it. Ha!

The more I write the Young family, the more I love them. I didn't think it was possible, but I've truly enjoyed this amazing journey to find their forever loves.

Thank you for joining me on this ride!!! I hope you enjoy them!

Love,

Elle

www.ellewright.com

Content Notes

Hi again,

I love to be surprised when I read a book. But I fully recognize that every reader is not like me. If you haven't read an Elle Wright book before, I feel like I should let you know a few things before you dive in.

IT'S NOT THE HOOKUP, IT'S THE CHASE contains sexual content, profanity, and sensitive subjects that some may find triggering.

Trigger Warnings include but are not limited to:

Cheating (not by a main character)
Death of a parent (on page)
Mention of cancer
Humiliation
Family estrangement
Grief

For Jason, thanks for being my very best friend and hero. Love you so much!

Dick Up, Thumbs Down

A DEXTER YOUNG ORIGINAL

Dexter

Part I

August, A Long-Ass Time Ago

*M*y mother always told me my gifts would make room for me. Of course, she was talking more in the Biblical sense. But I tended to think of my gift as sometimes good, sometimes hard, and sometimes nasty. It started right around the time I recognized the difference between my dick and any girl's pussy. Maybe I was nine years old, or ten. It didn't matter. What *did* matter was that most guys didn't think about feelings or a woman's intelligence or even whether they were wifey material. Truth was… men wanted to get their dick wet. Period.

The trick was convincing women that everything they'd heard is subject to change depending on the person, place, or thing they were trying to accomplish. Which I'd done successfully in my side hustle as a wingman for hire. I'd spent countless hours helping the ladies snag their ideal men—or vice versa. Today, I was on the job.

"What do you think of this, Dex?"

I blinked, meeting the waiting gaze of my client. Charlye Burke wasn't just any client, either. She was the one girl I've always wanted for myself. And I was a fuckin' punk who couldn't take my own advice. Hence, my current situation. Sitting on her bed, watching her try on several outfits for the date that wasn't with me. Instead of shooting my shot, I was helping her find the perfect outfit for the worst, wrong guy for her.

I shouldn't be surprised at this turn of events, though. Any shred of common sense seemed to evaporate with one look in her eyes or an innocent brush of her thigh against mine or the shine of her bright smile. It had been this way since we were kids, even when we were sharing a bowl of Superman ice cream, even though I was too young to know what infatuation really meant. Inevitably, I'd find myself drawn to her side during a family event or a game night or any other type of occasion that brought our close-knit families together. And now that we'd graduated from high school and were leaving for college in a few short weeks, my need to share her ice cream had been trumped by my need to wrap her legs around my body.

"Dex?" she called again.

Forcing my attention back to her, I let my gaze travel from her beautiful brown eyes to her bare shoulders, to the outline of her breasts, to those perfect, full hips, to her thick thighs, to her long legs, to her painted red toes. *Damn.*

"Well?" she prodded, twirling in front of the mirror. The clingy black dress was the exact right outfit for her. Classic and classy. Simple, but sexy. Just like her.

I cleared my throat. "You look good." *So* good. *Too* good.

Charlye grinned. "Really?" She tugged at the dress, then smoothed a hand over her stomach. Frowning, she turned to the mirror again and tilted her head as she studied her own reflection. "What if he says no?"

Unable to help myself, I rolled my eyes. Because *he* probably would say no. Because *he'd* never noticed Charlye. Because *he* was a fuckin' asshole who didn't deserve her. "He will." When her smile fell, I realized my error and quickly corrected it with a lie. "I mean, he won't."

She smirked. "Are you sure?"

No. I was never one to be dishonest, but that hopeful look in her eyes and the hard brick in my gut gave me no other choice but to lie. Well, not really. "If he doesn't see how bad-ass you are, then he's not worth your time."

Charlye rolled her eyes and slipped on her shoes. "You always say that."

"Because it's true." Despite what *she* thought, Charlye had everything that I—um, *any* man—should want. Beautiful. Intelligent. Accomplished. Kind. Funny. She ran miles around every girl in school. But she'd let her self-confidence convince her that she was subpar. I'd taken it upon myself to make her see that she was extraordinary. "One day, you'll believe me." I stood and handed her the sweater I knew she wouldn't leave without. "We should probably get to the party."

Thirty minutes later, we entered the party. Not too

early, not too late. The house was already packed, though. Classmates dancing and drinking, teammates playing cards and shooting pool, couples sneaking away to one of the many bedrooms in the house.

"There he is," Charlye whispered.

Following her line of sight, I saw the object of her desire at the table playing dominos. "Great," I murmured. "Do your thing."

She glanced up at me and bit down on her bottom lip. "I might need to take it slow. Maybe I should just go talk to my friends first."

Before I could say anything, she made a beeline for her group of friends. Sighing, I scanned the room, looking for my brother and sister. My parents had a lot of kids, but I was fortunate to share her womb with two very different siblings—both of which had encouraged and challenged me to do better. As expected, Duke was off in a dark corner whispering in an unfamiliar girl's ear and Dallas was in the kitchen pouring drinks for her friends and...

I held up my arm, blocking my little sister, Blake, from zooming past me. "What the hell are you doing here?"

"Shit," she grumbled. With a heavy sigh, she met my waiting gaze. "I'm minding my own damn business."

I pointed at her cup. "I see."

Blake rolled her eyes. "It's just beer, Dex. Please don't turn into a fun-killer like Tristan."

I took her cup of drink and gulped it down. "Please don't get into anything I have to get you out of, Blake."

Her mouth fell open. "You're so wrong for that."

"And you're so sixteen for that." I tossed the empty cup into a nearby trashcan and lifted a challenging brow, daring her to say anything else. Having seven siblings had ensured there was never a dull moment in our house. It also ensured that more than one of us had to be the responsible one in any situation. Since Duke and Dallas were off doing their own thing, I had to step up to the plate and keep an eye on Blake.

Narrowing her eyes on me, Blake folded her arms. "You make me sick."

I smirked. "I love you, though."

"You're not that much older than me," she argued.

"I don't give a fuck." I spotted Charlye closing in on her target.

"Who are you looking at?" Blake asked, standing on the tips of her toes.

"Mind yours."

"Is that Charlye?" Just then, Charlye glanced over at us, and Blake waved. "Hey, girl!"

Charlye grinned and waved back.

"She's so beautiful." She arched her brow. "I'm guessing you think so too?"

I tore my gaze away from Charlye again. Frowning, I muttered, "Take your ass home."

"Seriously, Dex? I promise, I won't do anything crazy. You won't even know I'm here. Especially if you're too busy paying attention to Charlye."

Blake would argue with me the whole damn night if I let her. And since I was already tired of this conversation, I said, "Fine, don't drink too much. If I even see a stumble or hear a slur, I will embarrass you in front of everybody."

Blake gave me a hug. "Thanks, brother."

I turned her toward the kitchen and away from the scene unfolding near the table. "Go away." I shoved her lightly, cracking up when she tripped over her shoe.

She stuck out her tongue and gave me a middle finger before she made her way toward Dallas. When I turned back to Charlye, she wasn't there. And neither was Logan Harris. Sighing, I decided to let go and get drunk.

"You look like you need this." Duke handed me a full cup of something strong.

I took the offered drink. "Thanks, bruh."

"You know my motto."

I shot him a sidelong glance. "Which motto is this? Fuck them hoes and get that pussy?" While we were "triples" with Dallas, Duke and I were also identical twins. We looked alike, but we approached life very differently. Duke thrived in a crowd, and I preferred to be around a small group of people—or alone. I enjoyed monogamous relationships and he avoided them at all costs. He was honest to a fault, and I was a little more sensitive to hurt feelings.

Duke laughed. "That was last year's adolescent motto, bruh. I'm an adult now, ready for grown man shit. The new motto is an oldie but goodie… You'll never eat if you keep your mouth closed."

Confused, I asked, "What the hell are you talking about?"

"You let Charlye out of the house with that damn dress on? The question is… What the hell were *you* thinking?" Although we'd grown up the offspring of world-renowned marriage and family therapists, Duke was the most talented of our group, excelling in every subject in school, remembering small details that we wanted to forget, and somehow knowing everything we didn't want him to know—and never letting us forget it. Just like my father.

"Man, shut up," I said. "Don't you have something to do?"

He shrugged. "I'm just sayin'. You helped her with her self-confidence. She walked out of here with Shitty Harris, and now she's going to bless *that* bastard with a taste. And you're just gonna… What? Drink a lot of liquor?"

I finished my drink on purpose. And I planned to drink several more. No sense in arguing with him or even trying to deny he was right, so I said, "Fuck you."

An hour later, I heard someone call my name. *Oh shit.* I jerked upright, realizing that I'd fallen asleep in the middle of the party. As my surroundings slowly came into focus, I noticed Dallas, Blake, and Charlye standing over me and some random girl snuggled against my side.

Blake shook her head. "What the…? Who falls asleep in the middle of a party?" She pointed at the girl clinging to me. "And who the hell is that?"

Sighing heavily, Dallas grabbed my empty cup and held it up. "Damn. How much did you drink, Dex? You haven't even been here for two hours."

I looked at Charlye. She didn't speak, but the tears standing in her eyes told me I'd missed something important.

I averted my gaze. "What time is it?"

"Ten o'damn clock," Dallas answered. She tilted her head to look at the girl next to me. "How did you end up with Cootie Trudy?" Recognition dawned when I took a good look at the girl currently wrapped around my leg. "I'm sure there were other women at this party you could've hooked up with."

I struggled to release Trudy's hold on my arm, to no avail. "I'm not… I'm not explaining shit to you."

Blake tapped Trudy's shoulder. "Hey." When Trudy didn't move, Blake shouted, "Excuse me?"

Trudy grumbled something incoherent and finally opened her eyes. Yet, she made no attempt to move.

Move, bitch!" Blake yelled.

Those were the magic words because Trudy let me go

and stumbled to the other side of the room. I braced myself on the arm of the couch and stood.

Dallas wrinkled her nose. "I'm so disappointed in you."

"I—"

"You need to take Charlye home," Dallas cut in. "She's ready to go."

I finally glanced at Charlye. "Are you okay?"

"Blake will drive you," Dallas said, snatching my car keys from my pocket. "*You're* obviously not in any condition to drive and *she* needs to take her ass home."

"I would've been drunk too if y'all weren't so fuckin' bossy," Blake said. "Couldn't even have a sip of anything."

"What happened?" I asked, ignoring Blake's muttered curses.

Charlye lowered her eyes. "I don't want to talk about it."

My stomach roiled. I tilted her chin up and searched her eyes. "Did someone hurt you?" Because if *someone* did, nothing would stop me from wearing his ass out all over this house."

She gripped the back of her neck and shook her head slightly. "I just want to go home." She brushed past me and walked out of the house. And I followed her.

The ride home was short and quiet. But my thoughts were loud as hell. I couldn't shake the bad feeling that had set in the moment I'd seen the tears in her eyes. All kinds of worst-case scenarios flashed through my mind as Blake drove the ten miles to Charlye's house.

Once we arrived, Charlye hopped out of the car and jogged to the door. I was right on her heels, though. "Charlye?" She dropped her head but didn't turn to face me. "Look at me."

Her shoulders fell. "He doesn't want me," she whispered.

I wasn't surprised at her confession. Still, I hated to see her hurt. "He's an asshole."

"He told me that we couldn't be together in public, that he had a rep to protect. He said I wasn't his type, too wide for him."

I'm going to fuck him up. I couldn't leave her like this, though.

She sniffed. "But apparently I'm good enough for sex, though," she whispered, hugging herself.

Fuck. Him. Up.

"I'm good enough to rub his little penis on my butt, to—"

"Wait, what? Charlye, did he try to force you to…?" I couldn't bring myself to say the words. "Did he hurt you physically?"

She placed a hand over my chest, right above my heart. "No. He only hurt me with his words." Charlye let out a humorless chuckle. "I guess I shouldn't be surprised. It's not like I'm a bombshell walking around here looking fine as hell."

I clinched my jaw. "Don't."

She threw up her hands in frustration. "Don't what? Tell the truth? I don't know what I was thinking wearing this stupid dress. I mean, look at me."

"I am looking at you." *I've been looking at you.*

"I should've known that he wouldn't want me for real. He's the star basketball player. He could have any woman." She swallowed visibly and a tear fell from her eyes. "Not me."

Unable to help myself, I brushed her cheek with my thumb. "It's his loss."

She frowned at me. "Yeah, right. You're just saying that because you're… you're Dexter. You can have any girl you want too."

I want you. "That's not really true."

"I'll probably die a never-been-kissed virgin," she continued. "Maybe I'll just get a cat."

"Charlye, stop." I stepped closer and squeezed her shoulders. "Do not let that muthafucka make you question your worth. You're not going to die a virgin. And if you choose to get a cat, that just means you have a pet. Nothing more."

"What's wrong with me?"

I brushed my thumb over her full lips, enjoying her sharp intake of air. "Nothing. The question is what's wrong with him?"

"Is it?"

My gaze dropped to her mouth. "You're so beautiful, Charlye." I leaned in closer, rubbed my nose against hers. "So beautiful." I kissed her then. Once, twice, three times before she… *shoved me away?*

"Dex," she breathed, her eyes wide and her hand over her mouth.

I stepped back, my eyes darting around halfway expecting an audience for my humiliation. "I'm sorry."

She shook her head rapidly. "I… um." She squeezed her eyes shut. "I have to go." She struggled putting her key into the lock. "I…" When she finally got the door open, she glanced at me out of the corner of her eyes. "Thanks."

She slammed the door in my face before I could say "see you later". *What the hell just happened?* Slowly, I made my way to my car and slid into the passenger seat.

"That was brutal," Blake said.

The last thing I wanted to do was talk about what had just transpired. The only thing I wanted to do was take out my frustration on the person who deserved it. "Do me a favor," I said. "Circle back around to the party. I need to whoop somebody's ass."

. . .

&

Part II

Summer, Before second year of college; Still a long ass time ago

"YOU'RE GOING to be okay, Charlye."

We'd spent the last several hours outside, staring at the night sky. She'd called me earlier that evening and told me she needed me. And, of course, I made myself available to her.

"I don't know…" she whispered.

I turned my head toward her and studied her profile. Still, so beautiful. Under the moonlight, she appeared almost ethereal. Her eyes were swollen from her tears, and her mouth… *Damn, I want to kiss her again.*

While my attempt to show her how much I wanted her last summer had failed spectacularly, the way I felt about her had never waned. Even though we'd both dated other people during our freshman year at Hampton University. Thankfully, our friendship hadn't suffered because of that kiss—and the subsequent beat down I'd given Shitty Harris that night.

She sighed softly, bringing my attention back to her face, her lips. "I just don't understand it."

"It's not for you to understand. Sometimes relationships don't work."

"But twenty-five years, Dex?"

I shrugged. "Those years must have felt like fifty to your mom."

Charlye's mother, Maya, had filed for a divorce. The older woman had finally decided to live in her truth and come out of the closet. Since then, the Burke family had been in a state of turmoil. Charlye's father had made it his mission to make Maya's life miserable and had demanded that their kids take sides.

"I feel like I don't even know her. Who is this woman who I call Mom?"

"She's still your mother, Charlye. She's still the everything she was yesterday, and the day before that, and the year before that. She's just not with your father."

"I wish I was as calm as you."

I shrugged. "We can't all be me."

She giggled. "I guess not." She sat up and hugged her knees. "I can't choose sides. I love them both. My father has turned into a bitter, nasty person. It hurts because I've seen them happy. Now, there's only bitterness. There's only heartache."

"Where do your brothers and sister land?"

She hunched a shoulder. "They're not saying much. Probably because they're busy with school and their careers." Charlye was the youngest of four and the only sibling that still resided in Michigan.

"I understand that." My own siblings were busy with life, and it had become increasingly harder to spend quality time with each other. "Maybe you could take some time and visit Elise before school starts." Charlye was close to her siblings, but was closest to her older sister, Elise. The two talked every single day and pretty much shared everything with each other.

Charlye didn't respond for several seconds. Then, she

glanced at me over her shoulder. "Actually, I'm not going back to school."

Frowning, I sat up. "What?"

"My head isn't in it anymore," she admitted.

My stomach dropped. "I thought you loved being at school."

She shot me a wobbly smile. "I did at first. The novelty wore off soon after the start of the second semester. I found myself sitting in class, zoning out, unable to concentrate. I flunked Economics, Dex. I just got a letter telling me I'm on academic probation."

"Why didn't you tell me?"

"Because… Dex, you're my friend."

The word "friend" hung in the air, taunting me. "Exactly. Which is why you should've told me. I loved Econ."

"Of course, you did. But you can't take my final for me. And despite what you think, you can't slay all my dragons. At some point, I'm going to need to figure this shit out myself."

"What are you going to do?"

"I've decided to move to Atlanta. Elise just bought a three-bedroom condo and asked me to come stay with her. Since I need a change in scenery, I'm going to go."

I stared straight ahead. There wasn't much I could do or say to keep her with me. Well, keep her at college. The only thing I could do was support her decision. The move made sense, after all. Her sister was there and so was her brother, my best friend Justus. "I'll miss you."

Charlye leaned into me and smiled. "It's not like you'll never see me again."

Searching her eyes, I leaned forward and rested my forehead against hers. "I wish you knew…"

She pulled back, a slight frown on her brow. "Knew what?"

"How much I…"

"How much you…? Love my cooking?"

I barked out a laugh. "Nice try, but you can't even fry an egg."

Charlye chuckled. "That's because fried eggs are nasty. I like my eggs scrambled with lots of cheese."

"Right." I knew how she liked her eggs. Hell, I knew her preferred breakfast, her go-to lunch, her favorite dessert. I'd memorized the little things about her, from the way she chewed on her nails when she was focused to the funny little face she made when she was too hot. She loved cottage cheese and hated beans. She enjoyed watching *Three's Company* and turned the channel every time an old episode of *Twilight Zone* came on. She was everything. And, although she was just moving out of the state, it somehow felt like I was losing her.

"Dex," she hooked her arm around mine and squeezed, "you'll visit me in Atlanta when you go see your godparents. And my parents still live here, so I'll see you when I come to town."

I brushed her cheek with my forefinger. "And you'll call me if you need me?"

"You know I will."

I opened my mouth to say more, to say what I hadn't said before. But I saw the hope of a new beginning in her eyes and didn't want to do anything to get in the way of that. "Good."

We sat there for a moment, staring at each other. The air changed around us and the heat of her body next to mine called to me. Helpless to the pull, I inched closer, my eyes laser focused on her lips. My fingers ached to touch her, to hold her. But…

Charlye gasped and hopped to her feet. She grabbed her jacket. "I should probably go." She pulled at her ear. "I need to make some travel arrangements."

"Tonight?" I asked skeptically.

She nodded. "Sure. The internet is 24-7."

"Okay."

"Thanks for everything, Dex." She walked to the passenger side of my truck and climbed in without another word. And I was left, once again, wondering *what the hell just happened*?

Chapter One

PASSIN' ME BY

Dexter

November, Last Year

$\mathcal{M}$y dick got me messed up! Every ounce of common sense flew out the window the moment I'd fucked Ebony Simms. And, apparently, my sense continued to evade me because I was still with her six months later. There was no reason I should've ever pursued her in the first place. Yet, I'd wasted time dating, gifting, pretending I could stand her... *This shit is so fuckin' stupid.*

"Dex?" Ebony called for the fiftieth time in the past hour. "Did you hear me?"

No. I'd tuned her out minutes ago. Work was busy enough. I didn't have time to coddle a grown-ass woman who liked to complain about something small every damn day. The sun was too bright, or the coffee was too cold, or the moon wasn't full, or the manicurist left nail polish on her cuticle. It was nonstop.

Ebony stood in front of me, her arms folded across her ample breasts. "I don't know why I can't go with you to Atlanta now."

The argument hadn't changed since Ebony found out my best friend, Justus, was getting married. I'd explained countless times that I was going to Georgia for a few weeks leading up to the wedding. Not just for wedding shit but because I had business to take care of and I wanted to spend time with Duke. The last thing I wanted or needed was to be tethered to Ebony for the duration of my trip.

I let out a heavy sigh. "We've already gone through this." *Over and over again.* "I have shit to do, work to do. If you want to come—"

My phone buzzed. I glanced at the text message that came through. I'd ignored the last twenty or more messages my siblings had sent, and now I was being threatened with bodily harm if I didn't answer.

Dallas: *Please don't make my pregnant ass come over and knock you the hell out, Dex.*

Blake: *That part.*

Duke: *Damn, Dallas. Stop acting like my niece or nephew will be here next week.*

My sister wasn't even out of her first trimester yet, but she acted like she was eight months pregnant. Which was surprising because Dallas wasn't exactly my dramatic sibling.

Asa: *Exactly. Wait until she actually gets a baby bump.*

Paityn: *And Blake just wants to fight.*

Dallas typed out a long-ass reply that I wasn't about to

read. Tons of laughing emojis and GIFs followed, then Dallas wrote: *Fuck all y'all muthafuckas.*

"I'm talking to you." Ebony asked impatiently, her hand on her bare hip. "Who are you texting?"

I peered up at her. "Can you get dressed, please?"

"I thought we were going to…"

Ebony was beautiful. Stunning, really. She was also successful, intelligent, sophisticated. Two weeks ago, I might've reacted to her offer with an affirmative "hell yeah". But she was a lot of damn work and the novelty of consistent ass had worn off. Because even with her standing in front of me butt-ass-naked, I didn't want her anymore. And neither did my dick.

"Nah, I'm good." I scrolled through the messages, reading all of them quickly. Before I could finally respond, though, Duke chimed in.

Duke: *He's probably fuckin'. Leave the man alone.*

I snickered. Fuckin' was the last thing I wanted to do at that moment. I typed out my response: *I'm busy, not getting busy. Get some business.*

The moment I hit SEND, more messages popped up, each one with various emojis and a lot of cuss words. It wasn't until my little sister, Bliss, spoke up that all the texts stopped.

Bliss: *Enough! This is dumb. Ebony can be part of Secret Santa. Damn.*

The conversation about my current girlfriend participating in our family Secret Santa party had been the subject in our group text for weeks. Dallas had led the charge, adamantly protesting Ebony's participation for no reason other than she didn't like her. Of course, Blake cosigned because she didn't like her either. Actually, no one in my family liked Ebony. Should've been a huge red flag, but that self-imposed period of celibacy that I'd taken to concentrate on my business had apparently rendered me incapable of recognizing the warning signs.

Blake: *Where's that trick, Ebony, anyway?*

I typed out the words "that's over" before I could even think about it. Then, quickly deleted it because technically it wasn't. So instead of responding to the final text, I locked my phone and sighed. "Ebony, we need to talk."

A loud knock pulled my attention away from my still naked soon-to-be-*ex*-girlfriend. When she bolted into my bedroom, I opened the front door. Blake and Dallas barged right into my house like they owned it and like they hadn't just been texting me.

Dallas plopped down on the couch and bit into a carrot stick. "You know I have no problem showing up unannounced."

"And I'm just with her." Blake shrugged. "Where's your girl?"

"We need to talk alone," Dallas added.

"I'm right here." Ebony emerged from the bedroom fully clothed. "What happened to calling before you come?"

Blake's eyes widened and I knew she was about to blow. My sister had always been a fighter. She never cared where she was or what she was wearing. If someone tested her, she was always ready to throw some hands. "Okay, so next time I come to *your* house, I'll call. But since this," she gestured to the room at large, "is my brother's house, fuck you."

"Okay, that's enough," I commanded. "Calm down."

Ebony folded her arms over her chest. "Yes, calm down. Dex and I were in the middle of—"

"Listen, Ebony," Dallas cut in. "We really do need to talk to Dex. Can you come back later? Or never?"

"Look, I'm Dex's girlfriend. It would do you well to

remember that. I should be able to hear anything that pertains to him. We're a team."

"Nah, bitch," Blake yelled. "I—"

"Blake," I warned.

"No." Blake pointed at Ebony. "You don't have anything to add to this conversation that I want to hear. If I tell you that I need to talk to *my* brother alone about *my* family then you need to leave. Period."

Ebony glared at Blake. "I'm so sick of you."

Blake grinned. "Good. Be sick of my ass and get the fuck out."

Turning to me, Ebony blew out a harsh breath. "Dex, I've talked to you about this before. You need to check your sister."

Blake's dramatic "Ohhh!" was quickly followed by her pulling off her earrings and kicking off her shoes. "Is that what we're doing now? Dex, you better tell your girl…"

"How about I just tell Lennox to come get your ass?" I threatened.

"I. Call. Foul." Blake threw her purse onto the floor and kicked one of my shoes. "I'm telling you… Y'all gon' get enough bringing my man into this type of shit. Don't threaten me with Lennox. I'll fight him too."

Dallas cracked up. "Yeah, right. I think you're looking for a different F word there, Sissy."

"Oh, shut up." She stuck her tongue out. "I'll do that too." Since Blake had fallen in love, she'd changed. Lennox had a calming effect on my sister. "I'm good, though. Too old to be fighting anyway." She tossed Ebony another hard glare. "You should be grateful because I would've dragged you all up and through this house—by your hair."

"I'd like to see you try," Ebony taunted.

Blake glanced at me, then at Dallas, then back at me. "See? I try to be calm, and bitches keep testing me."

"All of y'all get the hell out of my house," I ordered. "I have a flight to catch, and I don't have time for this shit."

"Dallas's phone chimed, and she answered. "Duke, your brother just kicked me out of his house."

"Probably because y'all are getting on his damn nerves," Duke remarked dryly. "Leave his ass alone. Call me when you get back to the house. I need you to do something for me."

"Bye, Duke." Dallas struggled to stand.

Blake pulled her to her feet. "Damn, Sissy. You're not even showing yet. Take your ass back to the gym or go run a mile."

"Shut up," Dallas grumbled, through clenched teeth. "I had a big breakfast." She turned to me. "And come on, Dex. This will only take a minute."

"You heard him." Ebony flashed a satisfied grin. "Get out."

Before Blake could get to Ebony, I stepped in front of her. "Go somewhere," I told my sister. Turning to face my girlfriend, I added, "That means you too."

"What?" Ebony shouted. "You're kicking me out?"

"Pretty much. This isn't going to work, Ebony. It's obvious that we're not compatible. I can't be with someone who gets on my nerves all the time. Most importantly, I can't fuck with anybody who disrespects my family. This is over."

Ebony stared at her, eyes narrowed, nose flared. Without a word, she pivoted on her heel and walked into the bedroom.

"That's what I'm talking…" Blake zipped her mouth shut when I shot her a sideways glance.

The room was silent while I waited for Ebony to come back. When she did, she had her overnight bag on her shoulder. No eye rolls. No cursing me out. No breaking up my shit. I half expected over-the-top theatrics, maybe even a smack or two. But she said nothing for a good minute and a half.

Finally, she turned hard eyes on me. "This is why I should've followed my first mind and went after Duke. At least he's fun. Maybe I'll call him."

"Good luck with that," Blake muttered.

What?" Duke shouted. All our heads snapped to Dallas who was holding up her phone so that my brother could watch everything unfold. "How did I get into this? Cause… nah. I told him not to get with your ass in the first place."

My sisters cracked up loudly, clapping and shaking with glee. Once Dallas realized they were the only two laughing, she sobered up quickly and said, "I'm hanging up for real now, Duke." She dropped her phone into her purse and shrugged innocently. "Sorry."

I counted to ten. "For the last time…." I managed to keep my voice low, even. "Leave."

The warning was clear and both Blake and Dallas rushed out of the house. Ebony, on the other hand, stuck around.

"I can't believe you're doing this to me." The first tear fell, followed by a steady stream of more tears. Then, she let out a loud wail and fell back on the couch. "I deserve better than this."

I couldn't argue with that. "We both deserve better, Eb."

She shook her head. "No. Don't try to be noble. You're an asshole." She brushed her hand over her cheek roughly and stood. "Fuck you."

Then, she stomped out, kicking one of my boots over and slamming the door. And I felt free.

"Attention, please!" The wedding coordinator shouted for the third time in the past five minutes.

For the last half an hour, we'd listened to speeches about posture and pacing and other wedding details. All of us were adults, but we also lived in different states. Some of us hadn't seen others in years, so the wedding rehearsal had been one big catch-up session. Which had, unfortunately, made the coordinator's job harder.

Justus slid onto the seat next to me and sighed. "Ugh… My head is bangin'."

I laughed. "Probably because you had at least seven shots of Casamigos last night." From the moment I'd landed in Atlanta, I'd been dragged to event after event— some with Duke, the rest with Justus. "Or it could've been the bourbon from the night before. Maybe it's that edible you ate before we got here."

He chuckled. "More than likely a combination of everything." Shrugging, he added, "Hey, I'm on vacation."

Justus had followed in his mother's footsteps and earned his Juris Doctor. Except, instead of attending the University of Michigan Law School like his mom, he'd chosen Emory University because he'd already settled in Atlanta when he decided to go to Morehouse College.

Justus groaned, resting his head on the pew in front of us. "Isis is going to kill me, man."

I scanned the room and spotted his future wife chatting with the coordinator. "Pretty much."

The couple had been together for fifteen years and had built an impressive life together. Early on, they'd made the decision not to let people pressure them into marriage before they were ready. Instead, they'd focused on career, travel, and savings. "She's so beautiful, man," Justus mused, watching his fiancée across the room. "I'm just lucky." He looked at me. "I still can't believe you broke up with Ebony in front of your sisters—and Duke. That's not even like you."

The change of subject wasn't jarring. It was just his way. I hunched a shoulder. "It had to be done."

"Not that it wasn't the right thing to do, though. She sucked."

I watched Isis point toward the back of the church and followed the motion. Charlye breezed into the sanctuary, holding a carrier with four cups from Starbucks. She handed one to Isis, then scanned the area, presumably looking for Justus. When she spotted us, she smiled. And my heart... *skipped a beat*? The years had definitely been good to her. Her brown skin seemed to glow in the low lighting of the church, her curls were wild and free, and those hips... *Damn*. Still beautiful.

Charlye approached us and handed her brother the other cup. "Reinforcements. Seems like both you *and* Isis got it in a bit too much last night."

Justus took a sip from his cup and moaned. "This is perfect. Thanks, sis."

She raised a brow. "Am I allowed to sit next to a famous author?"

"No," I joked. I still wasn't used to the accolades and the acknowledgements that had come since my book had been published. It was almost jarring because I hated the spotlight. "I'm saving this spot for a more important person."

Her mouth fell open as she laughed. "Not even if I brought you coffee?" She gave me the third cup. "For you. Just how you like it. Black."

"You remembered?" I smirked. "I guess you can sit down."

She sat next to me. "I've known you my whole life. I know the drill."

"Thanks. Hi, Charlye."

"Hi, Dex." She eyed me skeptically. "Are you sure you really need that? You don't look hungover."

"Cause I'm not." I sipped my coffee. Truth be told, I didn't drink much, not since that summer after our senior year of high school. There was something about waking up in the middle of the party with Cootie Trudy wrapped around me that cemented the fact that I didn't handle large amounts of alcohol well. Occasionally, I'd have a beer or a shot, but I preferred being sober to drunk.

"Good job." She touched her cup to mine. "Glad to hear you're still my Dex."

And again, my heart squeezed in my chest. Because I was *her* Dex. While it had been over a decade since she'd moved to Georgia, her presence had always shifted something inside me. No, I hadn't been pining away for her all these years. I wasn't *that* guy. My career and my family kept me busy. Other women had come and gone. Some serious, some… Ebony. Yet, distance and time hadn't dulled the effect she'd always had on me. "*Your* Dex?" I asked.

She nodded. "Yep. I'd hate it if you'd turned into… Duke."

I barked out a laugh. "You're silly for that."

She waved me off. "I love Duke, but he's a bit much." She leaned into my side. "I missed you. How long has it been?"

The physical miles between us had prevented us from seeing much of each other, but we'd kept in touch. A few texts here and there, comments on each other's social media posts, family events, the occasional wedding or funeral. What she hadn't told me herself, Justus had filled in the gaps. Even though she'd dropped out of college, she eventually went back to school to get her degree—after she'd become a master electrician.

"A year?" I asked. "Maybe a year and a half?"

"I'm thinking it's closer to two years."

"You're probably right," I agreed. "You look good."

Charlye dipped her head and took a sip from her cup. "Stop." She brushed a hand over the back of her neck. It was a nervous quirk. I'd seen her do it often, mostly when she received a compliment.

I let my gaze travel over her facial features, the blue rim around her pupils, her button nose, the mole on her upper lip… her mouth. "I just call it like I see it."

Justus cleared his throat. "Wait a damn minute. Man, are you flirting with my sister?"

Charlye blinked. "No."

I finally forced myself to stare at anything else, so I focused on the Bible sitting in the pocket of the pew in front of me. I shook my head and stretched my legs. "Not at all." As close as I was to Justus, we'd never discussed my feelings for his sister. "I think Isis is looking for you."

Justus jumped up. "Really?"

I barked out a laugh. "Nah, not really. But don't you think we should be rehearsing?"

"Right. We should probably get to it."

Once he veered off in search of some direction, I glanced at Charlye. The slight frown on her face had deepened as she typed something on her phone. "Are you okay?" I asked.

Charlye looked up from her phone. "It's Kelvin. He just told me he couldn't make it."

I was certain nobody would miss her boyfriend's presence tonight. But I said, "Is he sick?" She didn't answer right away. "Charlye?" I called.

"I don't know," she murmured. "I better go call him."

26

"Don't do that." Up until now, I'd made it no secret that Kelvin didn't deserve her. I didn't have to talk to her every day to know that she'd already invested too much into him—cooking for him, cleaning that fool's house. That nigga didn't even deserve a turkey sandwich with no Miracle Whip, let alone a woman as accomplished, as smart, as funny, as sexy as Charlye.

She met my gaze. "Why?"

"Because that's what he wants you to do."

"Are you saying this as my friend or as the Wingman for Hire?"

My little side hustle as a teenager had turned into a full-time career. And I made a pretty good living helping women snag their dream guy—or ditch their mistakes. "Both." I shifted to face her. "If you were my client, I'd tell you to stop making yourself available to him. You tend to drop everything for him, even when you don't want to. Make him chase you. Make him earn his place in your life."

"You think so?"

"I know so." I squeezed her knee. "And as your friend, he's not good enough for you. You already know that, though."

"Um…" she swallowed. "I…"

"Stop twisting yourself into knots to hang on to a relationship that won't last. Start thinking about what *you* need in your relationship."

"Whoa." She threw her hands up. "Tell me how you really feel."

At this point, I was certain she wouldn't be able to handle how I really felt. "Do you really want to know?"

The air around us changed again and a familiar tension enveloped us. Charlye must have sensed the truth just beneath the surface, the feelings that would probably never go away, so she did what she did best. *Retreat.* She stood abruptly. "I better go see if Isis needs anything."

Like every other time we'd gotten close to the truth, she bolted, practically running across the room to "help Isis". In that moment, though, I made a decision. That small interaction between us was enough to confirm what I'd known all along. She was everything, exactly what I wanted. She'd always been the woman for me. Now, I needed to show her how it felt to be respected, to be some-one's top priority, to be romanced, to be chased. And I was up to the challenge.

Chapter Two

YOU'RE NO GOOD

Charlye

S taring at my phone wasn't going to make it ring. Still, I couldn't stop picking it up. I couldn't stop the hope that surged every time a notification buzzed my Apple Watch. The only problem? Kelvin had yet to call, even after staying gone all night, even after I'd texted and called him multiple times since the rehearsal.

Stop making yourself available to him. Dexter's words kept ringing in my head, last night as I waited for Kelvin, this morning as I stared out the window looking for him, and now. Justus had requested one thing for his wedding—a family breakfast. Just us. My siblings and my parents. Despite the very palpable tension between my mother and father, we'd made it happen.

After I checked my phone again, Justus leaned over and whispered, "What's up, sis?" I plastered a fake smile on my face and was promptly greeted with a questioning brow. "Don't try it."

Growing up, Justus and I were called the "Irish Twins" because we were born less than a year apart from each other. I was the surprise baby. Apparently, my mother cried for weeks when she'd received the news that she was expecting again so soon after giving birth. As a result, I'd often felt unwanted, even though she'd done everything she could to show me that she loved and wanted me.

"I'm fine," I lied.

"I told you to leave that fool alone, Char," he grumbled.

"Are you ready for the day?" I asked, effectively changing the subject. "Tux, socks, rings... All of that stuff put up."

"Dex has it under control."

Of that, I had no doubt. Dex was as steady, as consistent as they came. While he was technically my brother's best friend, I considered him one of my closest friends too. Most likely because my brother had dragged me everywhere with him and, of course, because Dex and I were in the same graduating class. When we were teenagers, Dex had sort of taken me under his wing, protecting me from bullies, boosting my confidence. It was just his way. And I appreciated that about him.

"I'm just ready to be married," Justus continued. "I'm ready to make Isis Mrs. Burke."

"What are you two whispering about?" My big sis, Elise, asked. "I want to know."

"That's because you're nosy." Justus grinned. "I love you anyway."

Elise cracked up. "I can only be me." She leaned forward and mumbled, "Any conversation is better than sitting in silence for the past twenty minutes."

I took a moment and scanned the faces of everyone at the table. It had been years since we'd all eaten a meal together. And it showed.

My mother had kept her head down, picking over her scrambled eggs. Any other day, Maya Winters commanded the room with her intellect and her wit. Even her no-nonsense demeanor endeared people to her. Yet, today, she looked off. I knew that her wife, Julia, had been dealt blow after blow after being diagnosed with cancer several months ago. But Mom looked more sad than usual.

On the other side of the table, my father had spent his time looking at his phone and ignoring everyone. Which wasn't all that different from how he'd behaved any time we'd seen him, even when my mother wasn't around. He'd never remarried after the divorce and was content to be miserable.

The two of them had made a mess of their marriage and their divorce, and it had affected all of us in different ways. My oldest brother, Harper, had avoided relationships and practically lived at the hospital where he worked as a physician. Although he also lived in Georgia, we rarely saw him. Elise worked as a pharmacist, had married young, and was mother to my fave person in the world—my three-year-old nephew Ellis. I spoke to her every day in some form.

My father set his phone down and rested his elbows on the table. A move that he knew would irritate my mother. "You wanted everyone here, Justus, what would you like to talk about?"

Justus' frustration rolled off him in waves. "Hm." He tapped his finger against the table, then finally shrugged. "Maybe the weather? How about real estate? The law? Medicine? Electricity? Pharmacy?" His sarcasm wasn't lost on me, especially since he'd named off each of our careers.

"What about … Congratulations, son, on your wedding? How's my grandson, Elise? I heard about that ground-breaking research you're working on, Harper? So proud of you, Charlye, for getting your degree?" I placed my hand on his, but he forged ahead. "I miss you. How about a simple 'how is your life'? Better yet, can you at least act like you care a little?"

"That might be too hard," Elise murmured. She sipped her water. "Ellis is doing great, by the way. He's starting an early pre-school program. He loves to debate. Talks a lot. I'd say I have a gifted son. Can't wait to see what he does with his life."

Harper cleared his throat. "I spend most of my time in the lab, studying RNA virus evolution. I'm considering a move."

"Really?" Elise asked.

Nodding, Harper replied, "Both Vanderbilt and Michigan offered me a position."

My mother perked up then. "That's amazing, son. I'd love to have you back in Ann Arbor. So would Julia."

"Of course, you would," my father said. "You always wanted him under your thumb anyway."

Ignoring him, Mom said, "Please keep us posted."

"I'm considering starting a non-profit, designed to help young African American women who want to become electricians," I offered. "There's so much—"

"There's also a lot of money to be made in real estate," Dad interrupted. "The market is booming right now. If you'd taken my offer and come to work for me, you might be in a better place."

I lowered my head. My father had made himself very clear from the moment I'd decided to drop out of his alma mater, Hampton University. No matter how much money I made or that I loved what I did, he would never approve of my choice. Instead of supporting me, he'd constantly discounted me.

"Actually, she *is* in a better place," Elise said.

"You'd know that if you actually called once in a while," Justus added.

I love them.

Still, my father continued, "Where is Kelvin? Wonderful young man. Good head on his shoulders."

"Kelvin is not here because he wasn't invited," Justus replied.

I'd be lying if I'd said that my father's approval hadn't been the main reason I'd gone out with Kelvin in the first place. He'd introduced us at an event years ago. Kelvin's father and my dad were close friends, both working in real estate investments. Every time my father called or visited, he made sure to let me know that a marriage between our two families would be excellent. "He'll be at the wedding," I assured.

"Glad you didn't run him off too." Dad added.

The dig had stung. Sure, I hadn't had the best track record in relationships, but my father had this uncanny ability to make me feel like shit. I tried not to, but I slumped forward and massaged my temples with my fingers.

"Look, I'm over it." Justus dropped his fork on his plate. "I don't know what I was thinking wanting a nice breakfast with my family before I walked down the aisle. Obviously, I was wrong because—"

"Justus, don't." I placed a hand on my brother's wrist, halting what I knew would be an epic cuss out. Like my mother, Justus had no problem putting my father in his place. He glanced at me. "Please?" His eyes softened and he stabbed his fork into his Eggs Benedict.

Mom reached over and squeezed my hand. "Well, I'm

proud of you, sweetie. It takes a lot of courage to follow your heart."

"Why am I not surprised you would say that, Maya?" Dad retorted.

Mom let out a heavy sigh. "Charles, it's been almost seventeen years. When are you going to move on?"

Leaning back, Dad crossed a leg over his knee. "I've already moved on. Many times."

"You sure? Because I can't tell." Mom set her fork down, and despite the circumstance, I was happy to see the fire back in her eyes. "This is a happy occasion. It would be nice if we could provide the support the children need."

My father snickered. "You weren't thinking about *our* children when you came out of the closet and destroyed our family."

"Okay, I've heard enough, Dad." Justus pushed his plate away. "It's obvious you don't respect Mom—or me. Or anyone else at this table. At this point, you can leave— the state. Before the wedding. Because I don't need you here."

The table erupted from there with my father and Justus going back and forth. We were in a private area, but my father's loud voice had garnered the attention of several guests. Justus, on the other hand, had conducted himself calmly and professionally. Almost like he was in the court-room. He got that from my mother. Which seemingly infuriated my father even more.

Finally, my father stood and threw his napkin on the table. "I don't have to listen to this anymore. Enjoy your wedding. I won't be there. I hope the marriage lasts, though."

"Dad, please?" I begged. "Don't do this."

My father glanced down at me. "I've tried my best.

Your choice has been obvious for quite some time. I'll remove myself from the equation."

"That's the problem," Harper said, finally adding something to this conversation. "You're the one who made us choose. Why can't we love you both?"

Elise sipped her sweet tea. "Exactly. Your divorce made all of us miserable. And it wasn't Mom's fault. She's always encouraged us to talk to you, to maintain a relationship with you."

Dad glanced over at Mom, then back at my sister. "I don't have to listen to this," he grumbled.

"Don't you think it's time to move past this so we can have a good relationship?" Elise continued. "So my son can know his Papa. So that we can have a simple breakfast to celebrate a huge milestone in our lives."

"You've missed graduations, birthdays, promotions…" Justus shook his head. "All because of Mom. And I'll be damned if I don't invite my own mother just to appease you."

"Charles, we raised them to think independently," Mom said. "You should be proud that you have four beautiful, successful children. It's obvious this conversation is long overdue, but perhaps we can table this discussion for a different time. For now, we need to focus on Justus and his amazing future wife, Isis. I hope you reconsider flying back to Detroit and join us in this celebration."

All eyes landed on my father. Time seemed to slow as we awaited his response. Finally, he said, "Fine. I'll be there."

Relief washed over me, and I stood to hug him. "Thanks, Dad." Justus opened his mouth to speak, but I beat him to it. "Alright, groom. We need to hit it." I glanced at my watch. "You have a lot to do before six."

Both Justus and Isis had fought over which one of them

I'd support on the big day. She wanted me to be a bridesmaid, but my brother wanted me to be his best person alongside Dex. Isis won, so I was officially a bridesmaid, but also an honorary groomswoman because I'd promised Justus that I'd remain with him all day ahead of the ceremony.

As we gathered our things, I checked my phone one more time. Still no calls from Kelvin.

Elise stuck her arm in mine. "Where's the asshole really?"

I giggled. "Stop calling him that."

My sister couldn't stand Kelvin either. She thought he was full of shit. And that was saying it nicely. "I just wish you'd leave his ass alone. He's not worthy of you, and he's unworthy in general."

After we emerged from the restaurant, my father walked away without a word while my mother hugged all of us and headed toward her room. The hotel lobby was busy, staff buzzing around and guests chatting with each other. Since the wedding was in the hotel, we spotted several people there for the nuptials. Elise greeted one of our old neighbors with a hug, Justus walked off toward the front desk to talk to the hotel manager, and Harper ducked away from someone from our home church. To my right, another familiar crowd had formed.

Except for his older brother Tristan, the rest of Dex's family had shown up for the wedding. Currently, they were waiting near the restaurant, probably for seating. I strolled over to them.

Mrs. Young spotted me first. "Charlye." She squeezed both of my cheeks the way she'd always done. "So beautiful. How are you?"

"I'm well. You just missed Mom. She went up to her room."

Always smiling, Mama V as I called her, pulled me into a tight hug. "I already talked to her this morning. I'm going to help her get dressed after breakfast."

"I'm so glad you're here. She needs you."

Mama V flashed a sad smile. "I know. She's going through a tough time watching the love of her life deteriorate before her eyes." She held my hand. "Don't worry. I'll take good care of her."

The bond my mother and Mama V shared had spanned decades. They'd celebrated triumphs and supported one another through excruciating losses. Both women were role models to us and their communities. Through the years, I'd formed my own relationship with both Mama V and Papa Stew. They'd been stand-in parents to me during some of my hardest times and I loved them dearly.

I smiled. "Thanks, Mama V."

Elise joined us and we spent a few minutes catching up with the rest of their huge family—and their plus ones. I met Dallas' new boyfriend for the first time and got reacquainted with Paityn's husband. I'd already known Blake's man because we'd attended Vacation Bible School together as kids. Being around Dex and his family always put a smile on my face. All of them were hilarious, especially their father. Papa Stew had this uncanny ability to crack a joke without smiling. I had tears of mirth in my eyes before long.

Since I'd walked over to them, Dex had remained distant from me, talking to his siblings and Elise. Not me. Initially, I'd chalked it up to the fact that I'd been huddled up with Mama V for several minutes, but when I'd rejoined the crowd, he'd stayed far away from me.

My mind drifted back to the short moment we'd had at the rehearsal, when I could've sworn he wanted more from me than friendship. It wasn't the first time I'd felt that way during our long friendship. And each time, I'd bolted like a coward, afraid of my own shadow. In this case, scared of my own feelings. As much as I loved and trusted Dex, there was a part of me that could never fully believe it was real. He was an absolute fine-ass, perfect-ass gentleman in every way. He was my own personal angel, speaking life in my ear at every turn. Yet, I'd let that small voice screaming *unworthy* rule. Even though his scent drove me crazy. Even though he was my hero. He'd never lied to me—except when he'd told me that Logan Harris would want me even though I suspected he knew I was walking into heartbreak. I'd chalked it up to him wanting to boost my confidence because that's what Dex had done since I'd known him.

Unable to stand the distance between us, I bumped my hip against his side. "Hey, you. Are you done ignoring me?"

A half-smirk, half-smile formed on his lips. "I was just giving you a minute to catch up with the rest of the fam."

The sincerity in his eyes told me I was trippin' earlier. "Oh."

He leaned in, giving me a whiff of his cologne. Leather. Woods. Lemons. And something distinctly Dexter. "You should know by now that I could never ignore you."

Damn. That was a flirt. It had to be a flirt. *Wasn't it?* I blew out a slow breath, quietly willing my heart to calm down. "Right," I whispered. I scratched the back of my neck, picked an invisible piece of lint from my shirt, and stared at the painting on the wall behind him. All to avoid his gaze. "You never do."

"They're ready for us," Papa Stew announced.

Dallas rubbed her belly. "Finally. I'm starved."

"You're always starved," Blake murmured right before Dallas shoved her. "Damn, Sissy. I'm just kidding."

Dex nudged me softly. "See you at one o'clock?"

Nodding, I told him I'd be there. We'd decided to meet in Justus' suite for pre-ceremony pictures before we headed to the church. "Don't forget the ring."

"You know I won't."

Of course, I knew that. I just felt the need to say something. The Youngs walked inside the restaurant, talking and cracking up at each other's antics, while I checked my phone yet again. Despite the laughs and my still-fluttering stomach, I found myself tense and bothered by my so-called boyfriend's absence.

Elise gasped. "Ain't this about a…?"

"What?" I asked, whirling around.

She pointed straight ahead where Kelvin was standing outside the hotel—with another woman. Perception was reality, but I didn't want to jump to conclusions. One of the reasons I'd bonded with Kelvin was because he'd portrayed himself as a man who abhorred cheaters. He'd shared with me the toll his mother's infidelity had on his family, on him. Until now, I had no reason to believe that he would ever hurt me like that. As if he hadn't a care in the world, though, Kelvin grabbed the woman's hands and tugged her to him.

"That punk muthafucka," Elise said. "I'm going to kick his ass. Wait a minute…" She scanned the area. "Where is Justus? He'll want to wear him out."

My sister started to walk toward the front desk, but I pulled her back. "Don't tell Justus, Elise," I said. "It's… fine. I'm okay." Except, I wasn't. Not because I was so in love with Kelvin, but because I was once again the fool in a relationship. Tears burned my throat.

"Char, no you're not. He's," she pointed to the door, "an asshole. There is no way I'm letting him step foot in this hotel or to the wedding."

"I'll handle it," I snapped. "Just... stop. Please."

Elise crossed her arms over her chest. "Then, you better."

Tugging on my shirt, I sucked in a deep breath. "I'll just go and talk to him."

"No, you won't." Dex's low voice in my ear startled me, yet calmed my nerves immediately. I glanced up at him, noting the murderous glare in his eyes. It wasn't directed at me, though. Never at me. No, his ire was completely focused on Kelvin, who'd gone from simply hugging the mystery woman to tonguing her down like he wasn't standing in front of the hotel he knew I was staying at. "You will not give that muthafucka the satisfaction of knowing that you saw him. What you're going to do is go to the front desk, tell them you would like another room and instruct them not to let him know where you are."

"But—"

"No buts. You have shit to do that doesn't have anything to do with that fool. Because make no mistake, *he* is the fool here. Not you." A tear streaked its way down my cheek, but Dex wiped it with his thumb. "Once you're out of this very public lobby, you can cry. But not now."

I swallowed past a huge lump in my throat and nodded. "I'll do it," I whispered.

He searched my eyes. "You're okay." He wrapped his arms around me, and I held on for dear life. He must have repeated those words a hundred times in a short minute, but it worked.

Emboldened by his words and his instructions, I took another deep breath and pulled back. "I'm good."

"You certainly are. Now, we have a schedule to keep. Go do what you need to do."

And without looking back, I did just that.

Chapter Three

SAVE THE LAST DANCE FOR ME

Charlye

"*A*nother vodka tonic?"

I smiled at the bartender. "Yes, please."

The beautiful wedding went off without a hitch. The heartfelt vows exchanged brought many to tears. I cried more than I ever thought I would. Justus and Isis were officially married. And I was so happy for them. Really. Yet, after countless pictures, a full dinner, the fifteenth "*You're getting up there. Don't you think it's time to settle down?*", and the fiftieth "*You're next…*" I was tired—and a lot irritated.

The petite and perky bartender slid a fresh drink over to me. She leaned in and whispered, "I added a little more vodka and a little less tonic in this one."

I chuckled. "It's that obvious."

The woman grinned. "Very. But you look beautiful."

I considered myself a lot of things—talented, intelligent, funny, kind—but beautiful had never been one of them. My normal response to a compliment would be to downplay it, but instead I said, "Thanks." Because I *felt* gorgeous. The makeup artist had done her thang, without using a ton of foundation and extra stuff. My hair was styled to perfection, thick curls flowing down my back. The emerald green satin dress hugged my curves in the right way and the lack of sleeves didn't make me feel self-conscious. And my feet didn't hurt in these impossibly high heels. "I may turn into a pumpkin before midnight, though," I added with a laugh.

The bartender laughed too. "Well, make sure you at least hook up with one of those fine groomsmen. That's what wedding parties are for, right?"

I thought about what she'd said a moment. It might be nice to have meaningless sex, to get my itch scratched, but I wasn't the type of person who asked for it. Or even insinuated I wanted it. I preferred relationships to flings, even though my track record had been less than stellar. After the debacle with Kelvin this morning, though, I wondered if I should reconsider. Maybe it was time to adapt to the shitty ways of men.

"Char!" Duke Young slid in beside me and smirked. "Ready to get it in?"

I blinked, then panicked. "Why? Did I say something out loud?"

Duke placed his hand atop mine and squeezed gently. "No." He eyed the glass in front of me. "I was referring to your drink."

I closed my eyes and let out a deep breath. "Right. I..." I shrugged. "I guess."

He ordered two drinks, then turned to me. "You okay?"

I took a healthy sip of my vodka. "Long day."

"I can't tell. You're stunning, almost glowing."

A blush worked its way up my neck, and I ducked my head. "Thanks," I said. "I'm exhausted."

Duke smirked. "It's the music." Isis had hired both a band and a DJ for the evening. Currently, the older people were waltzing across the floor and enjoying the smooth jazz. Soon, it would be time to switch it up. "The good thing about exhaustion? It goes away as soon as it's time to back that ass up on the dance floor."

I laughed through a yawn. "You're definitely right. I could fall asleep right now."

"Shit, I already went to sleep. Dallas smacked the shit out of me." He sipped his drink. "Bossy ass."

I glanced at him. It was amazing how different, yet similar Dex and Duke were. While they had different approaches to life, they were both hot, intelligent, and caring men. "You've changed."

Duke eyed me skeptically. "Can't stay the same forever. Situations, careers, people…" He looked off ahead as if in deep thought. Which was surprising because Duke never really showed his pensive side. Clearing his throat, he grumbled, "Life has a way of changing you."

I tilted my head. "Are *you* okay?"

He shrugged. "I'm good. Getting ready to drink this liquor and figure out who I'm taking back to my room tonight."

"I take what I said back." I shoved him. "You're still a dog."

Duke wrapped his arm around me. "Char, men only do what women let them do." He met my gaze. "Remember that."

It was just like Duke to drop wisdom in ways that seemed organic. It felt like he was talking to me. I wondered if Dex had shared something with him. "Did Dex…?"

He shook his head. "One thing you have to know. Dex doesn't share easily. He keeps things close to the vest. Especially when it comes to you."

I frowned. "Really?"

"Really," he whispered, "and you want it that way."

I stared at him, mouth wide. "I do?"

"Pretty much. You mean something to him. He wouldn't betray your confidence. I just happen to be very good at reading the room." He picked up the two drinks and winked at the bartender, who nearly tripped over her own feet to pass him her business card. "You good?"

Nodding, I swallowed hard. "Yeah."

"Okay. Stop drinking at the bar and move around. People are watching you in that dress." The corners of his mouth quirked up. "Show them something."

I watched as Duke rejoined his huge family. Taking his advice, I left my spot near the bar and circled around the reception hall. Mom and Mama V were seated near the dance floor, heads together, talking. For the first time since she'd been in town, Mom looked happy, at peace. It warmed my heart to see her relaxed. I scanned the room for my father. When I didn't see him, I figured he was in the restroom or had simply retired early.

I walked over to Elise, who was sitting alone, sipping on a glass of wine. "Where's Jay?" My sister and her husband, James, had been glued at the hip from the moment she arrived at the wedding earlier. It was clear that my brother-in-law loved his wife's company. And I loved the way he loved my sister. "I'm surprised he let you out of his sight." I sat in the empty chair next to her.

Elise smiled wistfully. "He's checking on Ellis," she bumped my shoulder with hers, "and getting our suite ready for sexy time."

I cracked up. "Did you just say 'sexy time' with a straight face?"

"Shoot, it's been a while. I can't wait to get some alone time with my man. I'm ordering up no less than three orgasms." She kicked her leg up as she laughed at herself. "And it'll be so nice to have breakfast in bed, morning sex, and mimosas… just us."

I gave her a high five. "You do you. How long are you staying down here?"

She shrugged. "Not long. We're going to slip out of here as soon as Justus is too drunk to notice."

"I might be right behind you."

Elise shot me a sad look. "Why? You're too young to be going to bed early. And alone. Find someone to get under tonight. You deserve it."

"Says the woman who married her college sweetheart?"

"Shit, Jay put that on lock the minute he showed me his dick. And I haven't looked back."

Giggling, I finished my drink. "You're so stupid."

"Call me what you want, but I'm happy. I just want you to be happy too."

Happiness had always felt elusive, just out of reach. "That would be nice."

"And since you dropped the loser, it's your time. Did he try to call you?"

The hotel had acted swiftly and switched my room. It didn't take long for the calls to start. He'd left text messages too. "Several times," I replied dryly. Despite the voicemails proclaiming that he was confused, that he'd lost his phone, that he didn't know what my problem was, I hadn't answered. "I blocked him eventually."

"I'm glad."

"But you didn't have to tell Justus."

Elise shrugged. "I'm sorry. But I was still pissed when I talked to him."

My brother wanted to kill Kelvin. It had taken an act of God and a strong-ass best man to keep him from charging back to the lobby to find Kelvin. "Dex had to block the door to stop him."

"Yeah, I bet. He's so overprotective."

"Elise, what if he'd found him, beat his ass, then got arrested. How would we have explained that to Isis?"

"Good thing we didn't have to."

"Dex saved the wedding," I declared.

Elise eyed me, a smirk on her face. "That wasn't the only thing Dex saved today."

I nodded, then noticed the way she was staring at me. Like she knew something I didn't know. Or something I didn't want her to know. "Why are you looking at me like that?"

"No reason. Just… Dex is… Something about those Young men that make women weak in the knees." For years, Elise had an innocent crush on Dex's oldest brother, Tristan. But James had come along and changed everything for her. "I'm telling you… the older he gets, the finer he gets."

She hadn't told a lie. Dex was extremely handsome. Brown skin, light eyes, lean frame. Women stared openly at him wherever we went and some even threw themselves at him. He could've been the type to take advantage, but he'd always been a gentleman.

"Char?" Elise sang.

I blinked. "Huh?"

"What are you thinking about?"

I scratched the back of my neck and cleared my throat. "Nothing."

"Sure you're not thinking about Dex?"

I snorted. "Why would I be thinking about Dex?"

"Because he came in all Knight in Shining Armor, saving the damn day. With you and with Justus."

"Okay…?"

"Girl," she shouted. "Stop playin'. He's hot! Why not go for him? You know Mom and V always wanted a union between their children."

"Shut up."

"It's true. Why can't it be you? Well, it *has* to be you. Bliss is their only daughter left and Harper is not her type. A little too stuffy for her. And I love my brother, but he's a little dull."

Unable to help myself, I barked out a laugh. More than a few curious glances turned our way, and I covered my mouth. "You make me sick, Elise," I murmured. "Got me looking crazy over here."

"I feel so bad for saying that because I want all of us to be great."

"But you said it anyway."

"You think Harper is still a virgin?"

"My mouth fell open. "Elise," I hissed. And she cracked up—loudly. *More curious stares*. This time from the pastor and his wife. "Shhh." I pinched her leg. "People are looking. What if Pastor Wallace heard you?"

"Maybe Pastor Wallace should give Harper some pointers. He's been married decades. He probably knows how to put it down."

"Oh God," I whispered.

"Sex is natural. I bet you the pastor's wife is going to get some tonight. They got a hotel room. And the associate pastor is in charge tomorrow too? They're definitely getting it in."

The more she talked, the louder she laughed, and

eventually I dissolved into a fit of giggles at her antics. "You're so bad. We're going to hell."

"No, we're not. We're just having fun." She took a sip of wine. "And drinking."

I snatched her glass away from her. "I'm cutting you off."

Elise pouted. "It's okay. I'm already very tipsy."

Several minutes later, the music changed and Silk Sonic's "Smokin' Out The Window" blared through the speakers. At that point, it was on and poppin'. The lights dimmed next. Then, the younger crowd jumped up and made their way to the floor and the older guests headed back to their tables. Well, all except for my mom and Mama V. The two ladies were out there dancing and singing, hands linked as they showed off their Chicago Step skills.

"Look at them," Elise mused with a wistful sigh. "I love them."

"Yeah," I agreed. "I'm just glad to see Mom smiling."

Elise nodded. "She's so stressed right now." She looked at me. "I think we need to plan a trip to see Julia. It's not looking good."

I swallowed. "I know. Sooner than later."

Mom waved at us and shouted, "Come over here and dance with us."

We stood and joined them on the dance floor. Soon, all the Young sisters were out there with us. And, *Oh God*, it felt so good to just let loose and dance with people who meant the world to me. We stayed on the floor for several songs, laughing, showing off our dance moves, and hugging each other. I needed it. Hell, we all did.

When the DJ switched to a slow track, the floor cleared out. On the way back to our table, James grabbed Elise and tugged her into his arms, leading her back to the floor.

As I watched them dance, I couldn't help but smile—even through the heavy weight that had settled in my chest. They really were an amazing, accomplished couple. I wondered if I'd ever have that type of bond with anyone.

"Feet hurting, yet?"

I smiled at Dex when he handed me a glass. "Not quite." I held up the drink. "Water?"

"Vodka tonic."

I arched a brow. "You do know me well."

He hunched a shoulder. "Some things don't change." We stood in silence for a moment as the song played. "Just so you know… I'm proud of you."

I took a sip of my drink. "Glad you are because I feel like a dumb ass."

"We're not doing that, Char. Look at what you've accomplished this year. You got an MBA; you're considering starting a non-profit… You're a master electrician. How many black women can say that? That's bad-ass."

"Wow, when you say it like that—"

"Believe me."

I peered at him over the rim of my glass. "You always boost my confidence."

"I try, at least. You're hardheaded as hell."

"I'm definitely that." The song switched. Another slow jam. "Sometimes I wonder why I even try."

"To what? Be amazing? 'Cause you don't have to try to be that."

I beamed up at him. "You always say what I need to hear. I need to keep you with me."

His gaze fell to my mouth. "Just say the word."

And because I'm basically a klutz, I choked—figuratively and literally—spewing my drink on his shoes. I gasped. "Oh no." I grabbed a napkin from the nearest table and dropped to my knees. "This is… Oh God." I babbled on, spouting more apologies and more than likely saying other non-sensical things, while I wiped his shoes.

"Get up," he demanded softly.

I dabbed the napkin on his left shoe for no reason at all. There was nothing there. I just needed another moment to get myself together. My face was hot. Hell, my whole body was on fire. "I can't believe I did that," I muttered.

"Get. Up," he repeated.

I stood finally, fighting the urge to run. Covering my face, I admitted, "I'm so embarrassed." And something else I wouldn't name. *Flustered. Nervous. Attracted.* Even though I was all of those things in that moment, there was one emotion that eclipsed everything. *Fear.*

"I think being on your knees in a formal dress would be more embarrassing." He squeezed my shoulders. "It's clear. It won't stain. It's fine."

I leaned my forehead against his chest and let out a slow breath. "Maybe I should just cut myself off."

"I'll get you some water."

When he walked away, I plopped down on the closest chair. *I'm such a dork.*

"Hey, sweetie." Mom rubbed my back. "Something wrong?"

I peered up at my mother and smiled. "Nothing." I noticed that she had her purse and her shoes in her hands. "Are you leaving?"

She nodded. "Yeah. V is going to walk me up to my room. I'm tired. I promised Julia I'd FaceTime her before bed." She brushed a hair from my face. "You look beautiful tonight. I want you to have so much fun."

I stood and hugged my mom. "I love you."

"I love you more." She smoothed her hand over my head. "Call me in the morning?"

"Yes. I'll come up and see you. Maybe we can have breakfast?"

"That would be nice. My flight doesn't leave until early afternoon."

She squeezed my hand again before she walked away. Near the door, I spotted my father talking to… *Kelvin*?

When his gaze met mine across the room, I turned away. *What the hell is he doing here*?

Justus approached me. "What the hell is he doing here?"

To keep my brother calm, I shrugged and pretended to be unaffected. "Who cares? He's not with me. That's all that matters."

Frowning, he grumbled, "He's not welcome here." He started toward Dad and Kelvin. I followed him pleading with Justus to let it go. Only, I wasn't as successful as I'd hoped because he didn't break his stride—until Dex appeared out of nowhere and stood in front of him.

"Isis needs you, bruh," Dex said.

Justus stopped in his tracks and glanced back at his bride. He eyed Dex skeptically. "Does she?"

Dex nodded. "Of course, she does. She married you. She also needs you not to get into a damn fight in the middle of the wedding reception."

My brother responded to his best friend's calm demeanor. His shoulders sagged. "Fine. But I want his ass out of here."

"Done," Dex agreed. "Go dance with your wife."

Justus kissed my temple and headed back to Isis. I sighed. "Thank you. I'll go tell him to leave."

No." He blocked me when I tried to walk around him. "Let him come to you. He will. Then, you'll tell him it's over."

"I don't want to have that conversation here."

"No conversation. Just two words."

"I can't break up with him here," I argued. "I need to cuss his ass out."

"Do you trust me?"

"Of course, I do."

"Okay then. He'll come to you."

Sure enough, moments later Kelvin came to me. "Charlye?" He approached us tentatively, looking at Dex the entire time. "Dexter."

Dex didn't answer his one-word greeting. He simply folded his arms over his massive chest.

Kelvin looked at me. "I've been calling you."

I wanted to rail at him. I wanted to shout to the world that he was full of shit, that he didn't know how to make toast, that he loved to wear tighty whities, that he screamed like a little bitch when he was excited, that he had more pubic hair than dick. But I refrained. And I knew Dex said only two words, but I couldn't limit it to just two. "I know. I didn't answer on purpose."

"Why?"

"Because it's over."

"What do you mean?" Kelvin inched toward me.

Dex held his hand up. "I don't think so."

Kelvin backed up like the little punk he was. "Charlye, can we talk? In private."

"Nothing to talk about. I didn't stutter," I said, keeping my voice even. "We're done." Without another word, I turned on my heels and walked away.

"Charlye, wait." Kelvin's voice took on another tone, a desperate one. "Charlye?"

But I kept going. Eventually, I ducked around a corner and leaned against the wall. A surge of relief washed over me as I took several deep breaths to calm my rapidly beating heart. I'd never done that before, but it felt so damn good to be the one walking away instead of the one being left.

Seconds later, Dex rounded the corner. "Come on."

"What?"

"Dance with me."

I followed him without hesitation to the dance floor.

"Close your mouth," he commanded.

I hadn't realized that I was still gaping at him and did as I was told. "Oh."

Then he pulled me close to him and leaned down. "You did good," he murmured against my ear. "But you're not done. He's still here."

I tensed.

"Don't look over there," Dex instructed. "He'll leave. Two minutes." He swung me around so that my back was to the door.

As we swayed to PJ Morton, I allowed myself to sink into him, to let him hold me. "Thank you, Dex"

He lifted my chin. "You deserve better. But you have to believe that. If you don't, then you'll always find yourself with a Kelvin or a Logan."

"I know," I said.

He raised a challenging brow. "Do you? That means, no matter what he does to try to get you to take him back, you can't go back."

"I know," I repeated. "I'm done."

"Charlye?" He brushed his thumb over my bottom lip. He was so close that I could smell the bourbon on his breath, so close that it felt like a kiss. So close that I *wanted* him to kiss me.

"You've been drinking?" I breathed.

He chuckled and the sound went straight to my pussy. "A little. But not enough to make me sleepy."

"Good." I giggled. "Because I'm going to need you to stay awake."

"I got you." He pulled me even closer. I could feel his heartbeat against my own. "He's gone."

But I didn't care about Kelvin at that point. The only thing I cared about was the man holding me, the man making everything better, the man making me feel safe. And I didn't want to let go of that feeling. *Not yet.*

Chapter Four

Dexter

"*W*ingman me, please!"

Frowning, I glanced at Charlye, who was lying beside me on the bed. After the reception, I'd walked her upstairs to her suite, and she'd asked me to stay until she fell asleep. We'd spent the last hour just staring at the ceiling, talking about random shit, and not talking at all. It was our thing. Back when we were kids, we called it everything and nothing. "What?" I asked.

She finally met my gaze. "I'm assuming that's what you've been doing. Helping me with the Kelvin situation. Boosting my confidence." She smiled. "Actually, *that* should be your name. Professional Confidence Booster."

I chuckled. "Really?"

"I mean it. You're like a confidence coach, always in my ear, encouraging me to do some different shit." She snapped her fingers. "Like that movie with the man who feeds all the lines to the fine man who can't talk?" She kept snapping and pushing at my arms. "You know what I'm talking about. The guy." She motioned to her nose. "Long nose. He was in *Father of the Bride*." She struggled to stand up on the bed. Gesturing to the ceiling, she said, "He was in a tree or something. He had earphones so he could tell him what to say."

I raked my gaze over her—her emerald green toes, her legs in those shorts she liked to wear to bed, her plain white tank. I knew she was self-conscious about her body, her curves. To me, she was perfect. *So beautiful.*

"They were at the fire station," she blurted out.

"I don't know what you're talking about." Okay, that was a little lie because I *did* know the movie. I'd *seen* the movie. Right around the time I'd decided to become a Wingman, I'd binged on several romance movies with my sisters, from *Pretty Woman* to *Pretty in Pink*. I'd immersed myself into that type of shit because I felt like it would help me fine tune my already innate skills. My mother had always taught us to "study to show ourselves approved". It's Biblical, *and* true.

"Come on, Dex."

I smiled as she acted out another part of the movie with sweeping hand gestures and different voices.

Finally, she fell back onto the mattress, out of breath. "You know what I'm talking about. One of those 80s films. She was in *Splash*, with Tom Hanks?"

Finally, I took pity on her and laughed. "*Roxanne*. With Steve Martin."

"That's it." She beamed. "That's you."

She was right. I'd taken a special interest in that movie because it essentially gave me a blueprint for how I wanted to operate my business. Except, I didn't waste time with earpieces. Most of my time was spent coaching women for a date, whether that meant tagging along, delving into their past to figure out why the fear of dating was there or advising them if a potential date or their current man was full of shit. Which was why I worked well with my sisters. Bliss was a matchmaker. Once she made the connection, she often sent her clients to me to get them ready to meet their possible Bae. Blake was The Breakup Expert. She referred clients once they decided to break up with their men and I helped them close the door. My oldest sister, Paityn, was a sex therapist and… Well, let's just say, some women needed help in that vein too. Lastly, Dallas brokered marriages and negotiated pre-nuptials. While I didn't really do as much with her clients, she often consulted with me when it came time to evaluate her cases.

"Dex!" Charlye exclaimed, pulling me from my thoughts.

"Hm."

"Are you sleepy?"

"No."

"Sure?" she pressed. "You did have bourbon tonight."

"I'm good."

"So will you do it?"

I sat up and picked up the bottle of water on the table next to the bed. "Maybe you need to drink more water."

She gripped my shoulder. "I'm not drunk. Not even tipsy. I've just been thinking a lot."

I glanced back at her. She looked like an angel with her hair fanned out beneath her head, like she was floating. "About?"

"I've wasted a lot of time on losers like Kelvin. I knew he wasn't right for me. Nothing like I envisioned for myself. He's a dork. He can't dance. He wears flannel pajamas. He even sleeps in his socks." She pushed herself up on her elbows and whispered, "He wears briefs. Tight ones."

Cracking up, I said, "You're silly."

She let out the cutest giggle. "So not sexy. Then, he didn't…"

"Didn't…?"

Charlye had never been shy about talking to me. I'd seen her that way around other people, especially her father, though. I loved that she felt comfortable enough to share her life.

She sighed. "I guess I'm just tired of investing so much time into these men who don't do it for me. Do you know I've never been kissed until I could feel it in my toes? I've never even had an orgasm. I've been faking the fuck outta them since I started having sex."

The water came up before I could stop it, so there was no point in trying to play it cool. No, I just spit it out and lost all my damn cool points. "Shit."

She patted my back. "Are you okay?"

"Yep," I lied, clearing my throat for the sixth time since I'd spewed water all over my pants.

"You were probably drinking too fast."

"Something like that," I muttered, finally falling back onto the mattress again.

"Will you do it?" she asked.

It felt like a trick question. I rolled over. She followed suit so that we were facing each other. "Do what?" *Play her wingman or give her an orgasm?*

"Do what you do," she replied with a shrug. "I'll pay you."

"You know I wouldn't charge you." At the same time, I wouldn't help her get ready for the next man. Been there. Done that. *Not again*.

"So…?"

"What exactly do you want me to help you with?"

"I don't want to give a fuck for real. I want to be the

Charlye that was at the reception. In charge, confident, beautiful, sexy, ready to walk away from any man who doesn't value me. Actually, I don't even want a man right now. I just want to feel like I felt downstairs."

A smile tugged at my mouth. "You don't need me for that."

"I *do* need you." She searched my eyes and bit down on her lip. "I trust you and I feel safe with you."

Silence enveloped us as we stared at each other. One thing I counseled my clients on was following cues and listening to what people didn't say. I sensed she'd just asked me for something that went beyond the scope of a simple wingman. I'd been in business a long time and I knew when a woman wanted *me* to be their potential mate. But this was Charlye. Despite how I felt about her, she'd never asked me to be more than her friend. Still… *Here we are*.

I brushed my thumb over her chin and cupped her cheek in my palm. Leaning in, I whispered, "Stop me now if you don't want this." When she didn't say anything, I kissed her—so long and so hard, I couldn't breathe. I couldn't think. I couldn't feel anything but her. *Shit*. I poured every damn thing, every unrequited emotion, every unspoken thought, every missed opportunity, every wasted moment into this kiss. And she kissed me back with the same intensity, the same need. My heart pounded in my ears as I pulled her closer still, so close there was no space between us, no part of her body that I wasn't touching in some way. I didn't know where it would lead, but I didn't care. I wanted her to feel this kiss everywhere. And I wanted her to know that I'm the only man that made her feel this way.

I only pulled back to breathe before I captured her mouth again, sucking on her bottom lip until she moaned.

I couldn't get enough of her mouth—soft, warm. She tasted like lime and mint, sunshine and hope.

"Dex," she breathed. "Oh God."

"Tell me to stop," I murmured against her lips.

Charlye purred. "*Don't* stop."

Spurred on by her breathless moans, I tugged her shirt up and off. She immediately brought her arms and hands up to hide her body. I raised a questioning brow. "Char?"

With wide eyes, she said, "Can you turn off the light?"

I shook my head. "Don't," I entwined my fingers with hers and gently pulled her hands away, "cover yourself. You're beautiful."

Her eyes softened and she flashed a small smile. I circled her nose with mine, then kissed my way down her body, lingering on her mouth, the column of her neck, her shoulders, the top of her breasts, her stomach. Dipping my tongue into her belly button, I pulled her shorts off. I glanced up at her again, pleased when I found her eyes on mine, giving me wordless permission to go even further. I nipped the insides of her thighs and kissed the backs of her knees as I slid her panties down.

"Tell me you want this, Char?"

A blush had worked its way over her entire body, and it was stunning. Just like she was. She bit down on her lip and nodded. "Yes." She smirked. "Orgasm me, please."

Chuckling, I gripped her thighs and buried my face in her pussy, licking and sucking until she cried out through her very first orgasm. And even then, I couldn't stop. She felt so good, tasted so sweet, I wanted more. And more. And more.

After her third climax, she collapsed onto the mattress. "Oh shoot. Oh shit. Oh damn. I can't breathe." She struggled to catch her breath.

I smirked. "That's normal."

With wide eyes, she asked, "What the hell did you just do to me?"

"Is that a trick question?" I teased, sliding her shorts back on.

"Seriously. I didn't know…" She swallowed. "Damn."

I winked. "You said that already."

"Because it bears repeating." I pulled her up by her arms to put her shirt on too. "What are you doing?"

"Getting you dressed."

"Why?"

I smiled at the dazed look in her eyes. Honestly, I didn't know why exactly. I just knew that tonight wasn't the right time for us to take it further. And I always tried to follow my gut. *No matter how hard my dick is.*

"Dex?"

"Yes?"

"You don't have to leave."

"I'm not leaving." I covered her up with the blanket and returned to my spot next to her. "Not until you fall asleep."

The room descended into silence again. As Charlye drifted off to sleep, I thought about everything that had happened that night. I was sure I'd done the right thing by stopping this before it went too far. Because despite what *she'd* said, Charlye wasn't ready. I believed in slow and steady, though, and I'd perfected the art of waiting my turn. And I felt, in my gut, that my turn was coming.

"'BOUT TIME y'all asses got here." Duke shook his head. "You were on your way forty-five minutes ago, Dex."

"What the hell happened to y'all?" Asa asked. "You should've been here first."

I pointed at my sisters. "Ask them. I'm just the driver."

"I had to pee," Dallas grumbled, making a beeline straight to the food. "It's the baby."

That wasn't the only reason we were late, though. Paityn had to give Bishop a kiss, and Blake couldn't find her earring. *Sisters.*

"Oh my God, Duke." Dallas bit into a piece of bacon. "So good. You have a way with bacon. What do you do?"

"Fry it?" Duke quipped. "You're just greedy."

Dallas punched Duke. "Shut up. I'm eating for two."

Duke lifted a brow. "Sure it's not three or four?"

Blake gave Duke a high five. "Good one."

"All of y'all get on my damn nerves," Dallas said. "What time did Mom and Dad say they were coming? It's not like them to be late. And I'm hungry."

Duke poured me a cup of black coffee. "You might need this," he mumbled, low enough so that I could only hear him. 'Cause you look like you were doing something you shouldn't have been doing last night."

My decision to give my brother the extra key to my suite had come back to haunt me when I'd left Charlye late as hell only to find Duke had taken over my room and my bed in my absence. "Thanks," I grumbled. "You know what I was doing?"

"I could take a guess. *Char* and *Lee*?"

"I was minding my own business. Mind yours."

Duke barked out a laugh. "Thanks for answering my question, but not really."

Paityn squeezed between us. "What are y'all talking about?"

Picking up the conversation from before, I said, "Are you sure they're actually coming? Dad was hangin' tough last night." My father had practically closed down the reception. Even after Mom left with Maya, he'd stayed until the last song, talking with old friends and networking with new people.

Duke kissed Paityn's temple and went back to the stove. "You know how Dad is. He loves family shit."

"Especially breakfast," Paityn agreed.

My parents ate their meals together every day, even when they were traveling. Breakfast was their favorite, because it gave them an opportunity to check in with each other, and with us. As teenagers, we were required to show up in the morning, unless we were sick, at practice, or out of town. It served multiple purposes. The meal allowed us to check in with each other. Most importantly, it provided a safe space where we could get our minds right to tackle the day. As an adult, I appreciated that lesson. While none of us lived with our parents, we all agreed that it was a necessary part of the day.

Paityn hugged me for the third time since I'd picked her up this morning. "I really miss you." My oldest sister lived in Cali with her husband, so getting a physical hug from her was a hot commodity, especially since she was the nurturer of my siblings. When she moved, we all had struggled with the transition. "Bishop is amazing, but there's nothing like home. Nothing like breakfast with my sisters and brothers." She glanced at me again. "I worry about you the most. Are you happy, Dex?"

The chatter in the room immediately ceased and all eyes were on me. "I'm good."

Duke flipped the French Toast, observing me silently for a moment. I'd never really felt comfortable being so open about every little detail in my life. Duke was the only person I could share certain parts of me with. There wasn't much he didn't know about me, but the physical distance between us had affected our relationship in unexpected ways. "Sure about that?" he asked.

Growing up in a huge family, being surrounded by so many distinct personalities, I'd struggled to figure out my place in the group. Or even how to relate to my brothers and sisters. My parents had done a phenomenal job ensuring that all of us had an outlet to discuss whatever was bothering us. I'd taken advantage of that for the most part. Yet, I had a difficult time finding my voice. Duke had a natural charisma. He could talk to anybody, so he became my mouthpiece until I became comfortable in my own skin. Paityn also helped a lot in that aspect. She'd always offered an ear to us when we needed non-parental advice.

"I'm alright," I insisted. "You know I don't say things I don't mean."

"We know," Paityn said. "But we also know that you spend a lot of time helping the people you love, and you rarely ask for help."

"And you also don't actually say what you mean out loud a lot of the time," Blake added with a shrug.

The downside of being the kid of therapists and having several siblings who were therapists, was dealing with them constantly trying to "shrink" me. And since I was also a therapist, I recognized the attempts in small actions, various gestures, and other ways that they would try to get me to talk about shit I didn't want to talk about. Normally, it didn't bother me. I'd even done it myself many times. But today… I didn't want to hear it.

Paityn must have sensed my mood, so she rubbed my back. "Just checking in, baby brother."

I smiled at her. "I told you I'm fine."

Duke shrugged. "I keep telling you to move down here." Duke had been on me about my business, my ex, my life. My fault, because I'd let it slip that I'd been offered another book deal and a radio show. Since I'd recently published my debut book, *It's not the Hookup, It's the Chase,* people had been coming out of the woodwork to woo me with potential opportunities. And since I'd been in Atlanta, he'd been trying to convince me to move down south, to expand my brand, to build more wealth.

Dallas chimed in, "No. He can't move."

"X told me you met with him last week," Duke said, ignoring Dallas. "You still haven't told me what happened."

Xavier Starks was the current president of the Pure Talent Agency, which had been founded by my godfather, Jax Starks. My father and Uncle Jax had maintained a strong brotherhood since they'd grown up together and our families were tight as well. X was like a brother to me, but he was especially close to Duke. They talked often, so I wasn't surprised that my visit to the Pure Talent offices had been brought up in conversation.

"Because despite what you think, I don't have to tell you shit," I said.

Bliss raised her hand. "I would like to know."

Of course, she does. And because I could never tell her no, I explained, "I signed a two-book contract the other day. The radio show?" I shrugged. "Jury is still out, but I didn't completely close the door on it." I glanced at Duke. "And neither of those things would require me to move down here. Now, let's change the subject. Are we all going to the Starks' tonight?"

Thankfully, that was enough to switch the topic of the conversation. As my sisters talked about their dresses, I sipped on my coffee and checked my emails. I spent a few minutes, drafting a response to a current client when a text came through. From Charlye.

Charlye: *Thanks for being my first.*

After last night, I expected my next communication

with Charlye to go one of two ways. Either she would avoid me, or she would act like nothing had happened. The fact that she'd done neither confirmed I'd done the right thing. I smiled and typed out a quick response: *Always here to help.*

Charlye: *Good to know. Enjoy your breakfast.*

Dallas peered over my shoulder. "Who are you texting?"

I turned my phone over. "Why are you so damn nosy?"

"And bossy?" Duke said. When Dallas' mouth fell open, he added, "Close your mouth. Yep, it's your turn now."

My parents arrived several minutes later, interrupting the argument between Dallas and Asa about his inability to follow directions for Secret Santa. It wasn't long before breakfast was ready, and we were all seated around the table. Although Duke had vowed to never move a woman into his crib, he'd paid attention to his décor. And he'd ensured there was a dining room table complete with enough place settings to seat his entire family, even Tristan. Although, my oldest brother had never visited Duke.

As we ate, conversation flowed easily between us. We segued from sports to politics, from work to personal issues. Asa announced that he was considering opening a new boutique gym and Bliss shared the details for my niece, Naija's first birthday party in January. Everyone had their turn, and it felt good to be together. *Until…*

"So, did everyone else see Dex almost kiss Charlye?" Bliss asked, biting into a pineapple.

"Aw, shit," I mumbled, immediately pulling some money out of my wallet and handing it to my mother. I tossed my sister a side-eye. I would've expected Blake to say some shit like that. Dallas… she would've had no problem pulling my hold card. But Bliss? She was the sweet one, now she just talked too much like the rest of them. "Really?" I asked. "We're not doing this."

I loved my family. I recognized the gift I'd been blessed with early on. Life could've been so much darker had I not had their light, their support, their encouragement to follow my heart. But they were nosy as hell, and I'd had to set hard boundaries to maintain a semblance of sanity.

Bliss shrugged. "We definitely are. I just need to know... Why didn't you execute? I mean, she was right there. Waiting for you to make a move and you didn't."

I decided to go with ignorance, knowing none of them would believe me. "I don't know what you're talking about. Charlye and I are friends. That's all."

"Honestly, son, I wondered the same thing." Dad shrugged. "You definitely choked."

Mom shot me a sad look. "Hard. Especially after you came riding to her rescue with her shady-ass boyfriend." Mom cleared her throat and shifted in her chair. "Maya told us all about him."

Blake cracked up. "I'm just glad Bliss said something. If I would've said it, I would've got my ass cussed out."

I caught the high five Dallas gave Blake, before she muttered, "That part."

"Blake," my mother uttered, holding out her hand, signaling that my sister better cough up that cash for her cussing jar.

"Mom, *you* just said ass," Blake argued.

Mom shrugged. "But I'm not you. Even in Atlanta, the rules still apply."

Blake muttered a curse, but she picked up her purse, pulled a fifty-dollar bill out, and gave it to my mom. "This should be good for the rest of this conversation."

My mother tugged the ends of the crisp new bill and

nodded. "It'll definitely help me get those shoes I saw at Nordstrom the other day."

Dad leaned back in his chair and folded his arms. "Back to you, Dex. It's obvious to all of us. There's no way you and Charlye are just friends. The sexual tension between you two has been a thing since you were in high school. When do you plan on making your move? When you're fifty?"

"'Cause if you don't," Asa smirked, "I—"

"Don't," I warned. "I'll still kick your ass."

Asa scooped a spoonful of grits and poured it in his bowl. "I'll just finish my breakfast."

I scanned the faces of my family, noting the amused smirk on Duke's face. "Do we really have to talk about this?" I asked.

Paityn wrapped her arm around my shoulder and pulled me to her. "It's okay, baby brother. I love that you take your time with things. Maybe you'll get up enough nerve to step to her next year."

I choked on my orange juice. "What the hell? Why y'all trying to play me. You know I don't have a hard time talking to women."

"You definitely don't," Dad agreed. "Just *that* woman."

"Let us not forget the last woman you didn't have a hard time talking to," Dallas interjected. "Ebony was a nightmare."

"She was the pits," Mom said. "I'm so glad you broke up with her before Christmas."

"Dex, I love you," Bliss said. "But your choice in women…" she made a disgusted face, "sucks. You should let me hook you up. It's what I do."

"Bliss is right. It's almost like you enjoy a project," Blake said. "You get with these women who basically suck the life out of you and then you dump them when they don't color inside your lines."

Duke snorted. "That's a word right there, B." He clasped my shoulder. "She got you on that."

"I won't call you Captain Save a Hoe," Dallas said. "But you're definitely Lieutenant Help a Bitch."

Once again, they laughed at my expense. And, this time, I joined them. Because *this* was life with my family—always honest, always loud, always fun. I missed being with all of them like this, even when I was the topic of discussion. After they tossed around a few more jokes about me, my mother changed the subject to Christmas dinner and our holiday plans.

My phone buzzed and I glanced down at the screen. Opening the text message, I read quickly, and my stomach dropped.

Charlye: *Julia took a turn. Not looking good.*

Chapter Five

HEAVEN CAN WAIT

Charlye

ime is not promised to anyone.
It was something my mother had told me at a young age. It was her attempt to encourage me to take risks, to let me know how precious the little moments were with the people I loved. In hindsight, it was also ironic because Mom had spent decades living in a marriage where she hadn't felt seen, denying her true self because of societal norms, because she'd been taught that it was wrong to walk away. She once told me that when she made the choice to leave my father, it was the first time she'd chosen herself above obligation. Since then, she'd become an advocate for a woman's right to choose their own path.

My mother spent countless hours working to improve the lives of women of color, through her job as an attorney, her faculty position at University of Michigan Law School, and her work with the Color of Law Organization she was so involved in. She'd been a rock to us, to her students, to her mentees, and to her clients. But her rock? The person she counted on, the person she shared her life with, the woman she'd vowed to love in sickness and health, forsaking all others was… dying. And my mother, my Wonder Woman, was inconsolable.

The sound of my mother's loud wail when the oncologist finally uttered the words no one wanted to hear still echoed through my mind. Haunted me. I wanted to take the pain away, but I knew I couldn't. The only thing I could do was come. Several weeks had passed since my brother married the love of his life and I'd dropped everything to support my mother as she prepared to lose hers.

"Char?" My mother dipped her tea bag into her favorite mug. "Are you sure you don't need to go home?"

She'd asked me that every single morning since I'd been there. And I always answered in the same way. "I'm where I need to be."

"What about work?"

"I have a lot of vacation time." Because I never took time off. Every New Year's Eve, I vowed to take a trip or two, but it never seemed to happen.

"Thank you, sweetie. I know Julia is glad you're here." Her chin trembled. "I'm just happy she was able to enjoy her…" she closed her eyes and tears spilled down her cheeks. "…last Christmas with family who loves her. Thank you for frying her chicken for New Year's. She hasn't stopped teasing me about how it's time for me to crown you the queen of the batter."

I walked around the island, wrapped my arms around my mother's waist, and squeezed. "Don't worry. I'll give you my recipe." I kissed her cheek.

Mom chuckled and rested her head against mine. "Ha."

We stood like that for a moment. No words. I just wanted to hold her like she'd always held me when I was in pain. "Mom, I can't tell you everything's going to be okay, because it's not. But I can tell you that Julia loves you so much. She appreciates everything that you've done for her, everything you've brought to her life. If you ever wonder if you've done enough, you have."

Her shoulders slumped and she leaned into me, finally allowing me to hold her up. "I love you so much, baby girl. You have been a joy in my life. I appreciate that you're here. I don't know how I would do this without you."

Tears burned my throat. My mother had grown up one of six children. My grandmother breathed church. Mom had told stories about attending service every day of the week, being made to tarry at the altar by church elders, standing in line to get smacked on the hand for talking too much in Sunday School Class. To this day, my mother hated to take her earrings off because the church mothers used to make her do it. And once she was old enough to choose, she'd chosen to leave the organized church. Even after she'd married my father, who was the son of a popular pastor in the area, she'd made it a point to attend service only when she wanted to. And she never made us go.

Surprisingly, it wasn't until she married Julia that she'd decided to join a church again. The two had attended service every Sunday and were very active and well-loved members of their congregation.

With a heavy sigh, my mother pulled back and wiped her face with a paper towel. "I better go check on Julia."

"I'll do it," I offered. "Why don't you go take a bath? Relax a little."

"Are you sure? I want you to get out of this house.

You've been here day in and day out. Maybe you and Dex can go out to dinner, catch a movie?"

The Young family had been a huge support during this difficult time, especially Mama V and Dex. The two of them had tag teamed, spearheading an effort to ensure there were meals in the house and relief when we needed to get away. Thanks to them, we never had to worry about food. They'd also hired someone to clean the house and take care of the laundry. Dex took me for walks around the neighborhood, watched movies with me while I cried, and stayed with Julia so I could go get my hair done one day.

It had been weeks, but I still dreamed about his lips against mine, his tongue on my clit, the way he made my knees weak. His voice… I still couldn't get over how I'd shared something so personal with him with no hesitation, that I'd basically asked for what I wanted. And he'd given it to me.

When I'd texted him the next morning, it didn't feel awkward. There was no weird side hug when he picked me up from the airport, no stop-and-start sentences, no averted glances. From the moment I arrived in Michigan, he'd been the Dex I've always known. Which was both comforting and terrifying. *Comforting*, because I needed him. *Terrifying*, because I couldn't help but want more. We hadn't spoken about our interlude, but I wanted to. I had to know if it meant as much to him as it did to me. Not just the act itself, but the way he was with me—protective, tender, sweet… *He* was just what I needed in that moment.

"Babe?" my mother called, pulling me from my thoughts. "Are you okay?"

I nodded. "I'm fine."

"Did you hear what I said about Dex?"

"Yeah. I'll call if I want to get out."

She cupped my cheek. "I just don't want you to burn out."

"I feel the same about you." I cleared the counter of the breakfast dishes. "Elise will be here tomorrow. Justus is coming Monday. And I think Harper said next week too. Until then, I'll be here with you and Julia."

When we'd received the news about Julia, I was the only one who could come *and* stay. My siblings had all visited at different times, but they had obligations at home, jobs that required them to be there, families to attend to. Harper was single, but he was a physician. His patients needed him.

"Harper is coming tonight, actually," Mom said. "His assistant rescheduled his clinics for the week so he could be here."

"That's good," I told her. "He loves Julia so much."

Of all of us, Harper had the closest relationship with Julia. They'd bonded immediately, which had surprised all of us because my oldest brother had never been easy to connect with. He'd made it a point to fly to Michigan every month after Julia's initial diagnosis and conferenced with her doctors from Atlanta. He'd never shared that with us, though. I just happened to overhear a conversation he'd had with Julia about an event they'd attended during one of his many visits. The fact that Harper was arriving earlier than planned, told me that my brother thought it wouldn't be long.

Mom sighed and dropped her gaze. She ran her thumb over the edge of the countertop. "I know what you're thinking," she said softly. "He wouldn't change his travel plans if…"

I squeezed her hand. "Don't say it. Let's just enjoy her while she's here." I brushed a tear from her cheek. "I'll fix her something light to eat in case she's hungry. Take your time in the bathtub."

Once Mom left the room, I finally let the tears fall. It wasn't the first time I'd cried that day, and I suspected it wouldn't be the last. The more time that passed, the weaker Julia became. She barely ate anymore and didn't talk as much as she had even a few days ago. No matter how many times I'd told myself that things could turn around, my heart knew better. And I hated it.

Several minutes later, I carried a tray with cottage cheese and peaches, a banana, and her favorite tea to her room. "Mama J," I called as I entered the dark room. "I brought you something to eat."

Julia opened her eyes and smiled. "Hey, Pretty."

"Good morning." I set the tray down and flicked on the bedside lamp. "Are you hungry?"

She shook her head. "Not really."

"But you have to eat." I shifted her and raised the head of the mechanical bed up. Once Julia was released home to hospice care, they'd had to move her into the guest room on the main level of their two-story home because she required so much equipment and because she could no longer walk. And even though they couldn't share the same room anymore, Mom moved her favorite recliner in the room so she could sleep near her wife. "I can help you." I spread a napkin out. "Just a few bites?"

"No, Pretty." Julia met my gaze. "No need."

I swallowed past the lump that formed in my throat. "Okay," I rasped. "Maybe you'll feel like eating in a little bit."

"Ice cream?"

"Is that what you want?" We'd all decided that Julia could have whatever she wanted, even if it wasn't the healthy choice. "I can bring you Cold Stone?"

She beamed. "That sounds wonderful. For dinner." She reached out to me, and I took her hand. "Have a seat."

I sat down on the recliner and turned on the television. "What do you want to watch today? A Western? Hawaii 5-0?"

"*Pride and Prejudice,*" she answered.

I must've watched all adaptations of the Jane Austen classic fifty times since I'd been there. She loved old movies, but this one made her especially happy. "Sure. Which version?"

"The latest one."

"Gotcha." It didn't take long to find that version since it had been saved to the DVR for easy access.

We sat in silence watching the movie for several minutes before she squeezed my hand to get my attention. I jumped up. "Are you in pain?"

"I'm fine, Pretty. Sit down. Let's talk."

I did as I was told. "Okay."

"I love you so much, Charlye." Hearing her say my real name was jarring. She'd called me *Pretty* from the moment I'd met her, even though I'd acted so ugly toward her. When Mom introduced us all those years ago, I'd childishly refused to accept Julia. Not because she was a woman, but because she wasn't my dad. The woman lying beside me, though, never gave up. She swore to me then that she would win me over, and it didn't take long before she'd done just that. Now, I couldn't imagine my life without her. She *was* my mother too.

"I love you too," I whispered through my tears, because I knew this would probably be my last chance to tell her everything I wanted her to know. "I'm so sorry if you ever thought I didn't."

"Never." She shot me a watery smile. "I always knew."

"Thank you for making my mother so happy."

"I love Maya with everything in me. I was born to make her happy."

I lifted her palm to my mouth and kissed it. "I don't want you to go."

"It's time, Pretty. I don't want any more medicine. I just want to rest. But I need to tell you something."

My heart pounded in my ears. "Okay" was the only word I could get out.

"Look at me." I met her gaze. "You are worthy, my sweet Pretty. And you are so wanted by your mother. Never let anyone tell you different."

I sobbed openly. "Mama J," I whimpered. "You got me over here crying like a baby."

She laughed. "So what. It's just me."

I picked up a Kleenex and wiped my face. "Thank you for saying that."

"It's true." She cupped my chin. "You deserve every happiness in the world. My wish is that you find a love so strong, so pure, so tender… I pray that you feel his love so deep it warms you on even the coldest nights. Don't feel like you have to be on anyone else's timeline. And don't ever settle for less than you deserve."

"I won't," I promised.

"Promise me," she pressed.

"I won't," I repeated.

"I have a feeling your man is already in your life. You just need to open your eyes to see him. It may not happen right away, but when it does, don't run from it. Embrace it." She closed her eyes. "Take care of your mother. She'll need you. Make sure she knows I loved her until my dying breath and beyond. Be there for Harper. He won't ask. Justus, Elise, Jay, Isis, little Ellis… All of you are mine. I love you. So much. Remember that."

"I'll never forget."

"Love you," she mouthed one last time. A few minutes later, she drifted off again. And I watched her sleep until I fell asleep holding her hand as her favorite movie played in the background.

EARLY THE NEXT MORNING, while we were sleeping, Julia passed away. Harper didn't make it in time to say his good-byes, but she'd left him a handwritten note which brought him some solace. After everything was said and done, after the visitors left, after the house was calm, after my mother was in bed resting, I went to the only person I needed in that moment.

Dex swung his door open, and I walked right into his arms. He held me for a moment before he pulled me inside and closed the door.

Chapter Six

SHELTER

Charlye

 he ache in my gut only intensified as the days passed. Yet, I kept it moving because my mother needed me. Instead of planning the memorial, Mom had checked out and retreated to her room, leaving me to handle all the details. The only reason I was able to push through it was because of the man currently sitting next to me.

Dex had been present from the moment I'd gone to him after Julia died. He hadn't said anything that night. He simply held my hand and let me cry. And I cried—for my mother, my brothers, my sisters, and for me. Because we'd lost our mother. We never called her a stepmother because she was more than that. She was my Mama J. And I would miss her terribly.

Then, he'd offered his help. Since my mother wasn't in the right place to do it, Dex and Mama V had accompanied me to the funeral home to set up the cremation. In a few weeks, me and my siblings would accompany Mom to Hawaii, Julia's home state. While there, we planned to spread her ashes in the beautiful Pacific waters, off the coast of Kauai.

Instead of a traditional memorial service, Julia had requested that we have an intimate gathering at Gallup Park in Ann Arbor. Even though it was the coldest day of the winter, we celebrated her life under her favorite tree. And the entire time, Dex had held my hand, offering his wordless support and his warmth.

Later, a small group gathered at Mom's house for the repast where we served all of Julia's favorites. Because Julia thought every black funeral should have fried chicken. After too many forced smiles and countless hugs, I retreated to the guest room where I'd last spoken to Mama J.

The room had been transformed back to the state it was before hospice had turned it into a makeshift hospital room. Instead of the mechanical bed, there was a queen-sized bed. The oxygen machine was gone, the medical supplies had been returned, the medicine had been recycled. The television was off.

I ran my hands over the crocheted blanket at the end of the bed. It was the first gift I'd bought Julia. I remembered the smile on her face when I'd presented it to her. The woman who'd made it had messed up and I was so pissed. I hated that damn blanket, but Julia loved it. When I asked her why, she'd told me "I love that you even thought of me, so I'll cherish this forever."

A tear fell and I brushed it away. "You would be happy to know that Harper took it better than even I thought he would," I said aloud. I knew she wasn't there physically, but I still felt her presence. "But we all miss you. Mom's not okay now. But she will be. I'll see to that. I promise."

I plopped down on the recliner and closed my eyes. Several minutes passed before I heard a knock on the door.

"Come in." I opened my eyes to see Dex walk in. "Hey."

He held up a mug and a plate. "I brought you some hot tea—and a piece of my mom's pound cake."

I smiled. "Thanks."

He set the tea and the plate on the table next to my chair. "Take some time. I'll make sure no one bothers you."

I gripped his wrist. "Please stay."

Dex flipped his hand over and squeezed mine. He grabbed another chair and set it next to the recliner, taking his seat. We sat in comfortable silence. One of the things I loved about Dex was that he knew when to be quiet. And he was patient. He seemed to instinctively know what I needed at any time, even if it was silence or distance. When I was ready to talk, he would listen—not to reply, but because he genuinely wanted to *hear*. That made him a good friend, but it also proved he was the best person.

"I feel like Julia waited until we were asleep to leave us," I whispered.

He nodded. "I can see that."

Once I'd had a chance to sit down and think about things, I realized that everything that had happened the last few weeks of Julia's life had prepared us for this moment. Christmas, the game night, my fried chicken. Even that morning… she'd waited for me to come in the room so we could talk, so she could tell me what I needed to hear. The rest of that day, she'd stayed up long enough to eat her chocolate ice cream and have one last *Pride and*

Prejudice date with my mom. Then, she'd fallen asleep never to wake again.

"Is everything going to be okay, Dex?"

Dex met my waiting gaze. "Eventually. When my grandmother died, I wasn't sure how we would be able to eat chicken 'n dumplings again." He chuckled softly. "I wondered if 4th of July would be the same without her banana pudding."

"Really?"

"Oh yeah."

I tucked my legs under my butt. "How did you enjoy those things again?"

"When I realized that the most important thing was the family time. My mother knows how to make banana pudding. Paityn's chicken 'n dumplings are good as hell. In some ways, better than Granny's. The food just brought us together. But the time we spent, the memories, the laughter…it's still here. She's still with me. Her impact on my life is eternal."

"I just miss her." I breathed.

"You'll always miss her, but eventually, you'll be able to smile through your tears because you'll remember something funny or just feel extremely grateful that you were blessed to have her for as long as you did."

More tears fell. "I just… She said some things to me the morning before she died. I can't stop thinking about it."

"Knowing Julia, I would say that's exactly the effect she wanted to have."

I laughed softly. "You're right. She was very intentional."

"Exactly."

"I feel so lost. I don't know what to do."

"You don't have to *do* anything right now, Charlye.

There's no set timetable for grief. Just feel it. Whatever it is… It's not wrong."

I stared at him, took him in. He'd paired black slacks with a black turtleneck. Cool, yet understated. Even when he wasn't trying, he looked so damn fine. "Thank you."

"Stop thanking me. You're good."

I broke a piece of the cake off and tasted it. "This is slappin'."

He chuckled. "As always."

"Share with me?"

"I can only eat my mama's cake with milk."

"You can have some of my tea."

"Pound cake and tea… Nah, I'm good."

"Man, bye!" I argued. "You don't know what you're missing. Julia turned me on to the combination. Changed my life."

"Key words… *Your* life."

I laughed and it felt like a weight had been lifted. "Whatever." I ate another piece of cake and sipped my tea. "Sit there and watch me, then. How about that?"

He smirked. "I'm good with that."

When I finished my slice, I let out a heavy sigh. "I guess I better show my face, check on Mom."

Dex stood. "Ready when you are."

I took his outstretched hand and let him pull me to my feet. Peering up at him, I clutched his sweater with my fist. "Thanks for everything." My eyes dropped to his mouth. "I appreciate you."

He smiled. "You know I got you."

"You do, don't you?"

"Always." He wrapped his arms around my waist and pulled me close to him. "You never have to ask."

The haze of grief had pretty much ensured that our conversations had been solely centered on me, what I needed and what my family needed. Dex had availed himself to all of us and I was grateful. At the same time, it almost felt like our interlude the night of the wedding had been a bomb-ass dream. Even though I still remembered everything about that night, Dex seemed unphased. I should've been happy that things weren't awkward. And I was. Yet… part of me wanted him to be a little uncomfortable. After years of friendship, we'd crossed a line. We deliberately walked into unchartered territory, and I couldn't stop thinking about it, or imagining what it would've been like to be with him entirely. *Did he feel the same way?*

Maybe it was because I didn't quite trust myself with him or with anyone for that matter? My last several relationships had ended with hurt feelings. Namely, mine. Maybe I was hesitant because there was still a part of me that didn't quite believe he could want me? I mean… he hadn't mentioned it since. He'd been there, but he hadn't tried to cop a feel, kiss me, or even… *What if he gave me a pity orgasm?*

The best thing to do would be to ask. Yet, for some reason, I was completely comfortable beating around the bush with Dex. All that bravado that prompted me to ask him to make me come had disappeared. I couldn't even bring myself to ask him to kiss me. And I couldn't kiss him. A therapist might call it fear of rejection, but I just called it scared as hell.

But this was Dex. He was one of the best people I knew. Logically, I knew we would be okay after we had the conversation because I trusted him. But…

"What's wrong?" he asked, pulling me from my thoughts.

I bit down on my lip and decided to just say it. "Why is that?" He raised a questioning brow and I continued,

"Why are you always here for me?" I leaned my forehead against his warm chest. "Never mind. That sounded stupid."

He chuckled. "Char?"

Damn, his voice... The way he said my name. I hadn't noticed before, but it was endearing, seductive. "Hot."

He frowned. "Hot?"

Shit. Without looking at him, I said, "It's hot."

I pray that you feel his love so deep it warms you on even the coldest nights. Julia's words replayed through my mind on an endless loop. Everything seemed to click. She'd told me that she suspected that my man was someone I already knew. Could she have been referring to Dex? The bitter cold of the morning hadn't penetrated because he'd sheltered me. He'd lent me some of his warmth.

"You're hot," I whispered.

He smirked. "Okay?"

"I mean, your body heat. It's... hot," I stammered. "I never feel cold when you're around. It just reminded me of something Julia told me."

"Did you want to ask me something?"

I shook my head. "No. I didn't want to ask you anything? I just... I want..." Since I obviously couldn't use my words, I kissed him.

For the past few days, I'd experienced several emotions, but grief had been the dominant one. With one touch of his lips to mine, every tear, every ache, all the sadness disappeared. I welcomed the flood of excitement and desire mixed with adoration and lust. The intense hum in my veins, the pounding of my heart in my ears made me feel free, alive. I wanted to bottle this feeling, I wanted to tuck it in my pocket and keep it with me forever. *I wanted him.*

My legs shook and I thought they would buckle, but his

strong arm held me up, cradling me against him. Licking. Kissing. Sucking. I shuddered when he moaned my name, I trembled when he gripped my hair in his fist and pulled me closer. I feathered my fingers over the waist of his pants, tempted to take it further, tempted to pull him back on the mattress so he could ease the ache in my core. He was everything, and I wanted nothing more than to hold on to him.

My fingers lingered over the button of his slacks. "Tell me to stop," I whispered against his lips.

He shook his head and pressed his mouth to mine. But before I could follow through, before I could drop to my knees and taste him, a soft knock on the door dampened the haze.

"Damn." He rested his forehead against mine and muttered another dark curse.

I stared at him through hooded eyes. "Do we have to get that?"

Another knock. "Char?" Elise called from the other side of the door. Dex backed away right before she cracked the door open and poked her head in. She smiled and stepped into the room. "You're here. We've been looking for you. What have you…?" Her eyes darted back and forth between Dex and me, and a slow smirk spread across her lips. "Shoot." She snapped her fingers. "I just remembered where the blender was. I thought I needed you, but now I don't. I'll just… go get it."

Justus walked into the room. "Char, where the hell have you been?" He glanced at Dex, then back at me. Then, at Dex. "What's going on in here?

Elise tugged on Justus' arm. "Come on. Help me in the kitchen."

Frowning, Justus stared at Dex, but addressed me, "You good, Char? Why is your face so flushed?"

"Why are you so damn nosy?" Elise asked.

I let out a breathless giggle. "I'm fine, Justus. Dex was just listening to me cry for the umpteenth time today," I lied.

Harper entered next. "Mom's been looking for you, Char. The guests are leaving." He gave Dex dap. "I didn't know you were still here. V is looking for you too."

Dex shot me a sidelong glance. "I better go see what she wants."

Harper followed him out of the room, leaving me with Justus and Elise. I pointed at the door. "I'll be out in a minute."

Justus squeezed my shoulders and placed a kiss to my forehead. "Love you. We're going to be okay."

I nodded. "Love you too."

When my brother left, Elise practically skipped over to me. "I want to know every damn thing that happened in this room while I was stuck out there with all those people eating fried chicken and promising to keep in touch knowing they won't. I mean it, Char. Every damn detail."

"We have to go," I told her. "You heard Harper."

"Did I walk in before you took your clothes off or after you put them back on?" I'd made the mistake of telling Elise about the gift Dex had given me the night of the wedding. "I need to know if the dick finally came out of the pants."

"Why do you need to know that?"

"Because I'm nosy as hell. You already know that."

I pushed my big sister toward the door. "Get out of here, fool. I'm not telling you anything."

Elise argued with me all the way to the kitchen. "When everyone leaves, we're having a heart to heart."

"No, we're not," I said.

The kitchen was empty when we stepped in the room,

which seemed odd. Elise looked at me, a frown on her face. "Where is everybody?"

I shrugged. "Maybe they left."

"I'm pretty sure everybody didn't leave. Dex was just here. And V said she was staying the night." She disappeared into the living room.

When she didn't come back, I followed her. I spotted Mom first, then Justus and Harper. To my right, Dex and Mama V were standing there. And my... "Dad?"

My father smiled sadly. "Hi, Charlye."

I hadn't seen my father since the wedding. He hadn't called during the holidays, hadn't reached out to give condolences. Anger welled up inside. We needed him and he'd failed yet again to be there for us. Glaring at him, I said, "What the hell are you doing here?"

IT TOOK a few minutes to clear out the house after my father showed up, but we finally said our goodbyes to the people who'd actually been there for us. Mama V had stayed behind only because Mom asked her to stay. But she'd excused herself from the room, leaving us alone with my father.

"You might want to think about what you say today, Dad," Harper warned, his voice low.

For the first time, I noticed that my father had been clutching his hat in one hand and an envelope in the other. Nodding, Dad said, "I'm not here to start a fight." He handed my mother the envelope. "I wanted to drop this off for you."

Mom eyed him skeptically. She had every right not to trust a word my father said, but she opened it anyway. Scanning the contents quickly, she closed her eyes and held the card against her chest. Tears spilled from her eyes.

"What is it, Mom?" Elise asked, her voice thick with unshed tears.

Mom handed Elise the card. After she read it, she gasped. "Oh my God."

Justus took the card from her. It didn't take long for him to scan it and give it to Harper who read with interest. Then, he broke down in tears as well. My mother walked over to him and pulled him into a hug. I was the last one to read it. It was from Julia.

My dearest family,

Thank you for bringing me so much joy. Before I met you, I never knew what it was like to love someone unconditionally. Growing up, I didn't have loving parents. I spent so much of my time alone. I couldn't fathom a life with family dinners, game nights, and picnics. But you all have given me that, and so much more.

From the moment I met you, I've never felt lonely again. Thank you for showing me that life is beautiful, that love is healing. I know you're hurting. For that, I'm sorry. I hate that I'm not there to comfort you. But I'm not sorry that I love you, that I was able to be an important part of your lives.

Now, for my final wish… I'm sending this letter to Charles with hope that he'll bring it to you. True healing can begin with an honest conversation. I don't expect it to happen overnight, but I do expect you to try.

Be good to each other. Love one another even when it's hard.

I love you all so much.

J

I sat down on the arm of the couch and dropped my head. I felt Justus' strong hand on my shoulder.

"I'm sorry," Dad whispered. I looked up then, noticed the tears standing in his eyes. "I'm truly sorry for your loss."

Harper embraced my father then, prompting all of us to go to him. Even Mom. We stood like that for a moment, arms wrapped around each other, tears flowing from our eyes. Even in death, Julia had worked one last miracle. We had a lot of work to do. There was so much that needed to be discussed, so many harsh words and empty promises that had to be overcome. But the despair that had consumed us even a few minutes ago had been replaced with new mercy, new hope. And, for the first time in a long time, I knew that everything would be alright.

Chapter Seven

DISTANCE

Dexter

By the time I arrived at my parents' house for my niece Naija's birthday party, there were several guests already there. Children were running around and screaming for no reason, Bliss' mom friends were talking about terrible twos and breast milk, and Mom was effortlessly greeting everyone with warm hugs and wide smiles.

One kid zoomed past me and jumped into a mini ball pit, and Asa was chasing another kid who'd stolen his iPhone. To my right, Paityn held a baby in her arms, rocking him to sleep, while she yapped with someone who I assumed was the mother. A random kid smacked my shin when I stepped on a piece of paper they were playing with. And another strange little person dipped his finger in a plate that had been left unattended on the coffee table. I expected the party to be kind of low-key, more adults than

children. After all, it was only Naija's first birthday. But...
Who the hell are all these kids?

"Up!"

I felt a tiny palm tug on my jeans and glanced down. Grinning, I scooped my niece, Naija, up in my arms. She flashed her beautiful smile and set a half-eaten piece of banana in my hand. "Is this mine?" I asked.

She frowned. "Naty."

I chuckled. "It's nasty?"

She nodded. "Mm hmm."

I pointed to my cheek. "Give me a kiss." She brushed her sticky lips on my face and blew. It was our thing, so I repeated the gesture on her cheek. "What's my name?"

"Hm?"

"Say Uncle Dexter?"

She mumbled something incoherent, then pointed at the ground.

When she was born, we'd placed bets on whose name she said first. Blake won, even though she pronounced it "Bake". I wanted to be next. "Can you say Uncle?"

"Unca!" she shouted.

"Dexter."

"Dickta," she muttered.

I chuckled. "That's good enough, baby doll." I kissed her cheek again. "Happy Birthday."

"Uh oh." She held up her finger and a tiny bit of banana was still on it. She shook her head. "No." Then, she smeared it on my palm.

"Thanks," I grumbled, looking around for a napkin.

She lifted her hand and attempted to wave at me, but it looked more like she was throwing up a gang sign. "Bye, Bye." I took that as my cue that she was done with me, so, I put her down.

Blake walked over, munching on some chips. "I guess

she told you, brotha. Gave you her nasty leftovers and ran away." She cracked up. "I might be able to teach her a few things."

"No, I think she meant to give it to you." I dropped the soggy banana in her bowl right on top of the chip I knew she was saving 'til last and snatched her napkin out of her hand. My sister was very particular about how she ate her food and where she ate. She rarely mixed food, hated buffets, and liked to save the best for last.

Blake screeched, "Fuck!"

"Blake!" My mother motioned to the little girl currently staring at Blake. "Little ears. And run me my money."

"I guess she told you," I mocked.

"I wanted that chip." Blake smacked me and whispered under her breath, "muthafucka."

Wrapping my arm around her, I kissed her temple. "I love you too."

Blake finally acknowledged her little admirer. "Can I help you?" she asked the little girl.

"Are you a bitch?" the girl asked. "My dad said only bitches hit people."

I cracked up at the blush that worked its way up my usually unflappable and unbothered sister.

Blake glared at me, then asked the girl, "Who's your daddy, baby? Is he here?"

"My name is Pilar," the girl corrected. "Not baby."

My sister took a deep breath. "Okay, Pilar. Where's your father?"

"My Mommie said he couldn't come to this party because…" She blew out a deep breath and bit into an iced pretzel. "…hoes would be here."

"Whose kid is this?" Blake asked loudly. "Somebody come get this lil' girl."

A woman rushed over, apologizing profusely, before she whisked the very inquisitive and a-little-too-grown-for-her-age cutie pie away.

Blake stared after the little girl with an annoyed look on her face. "Who the fuck is that?" she grumbled. "I told Bliss about bringing home strays. See this?" She signed the letter "E".

"E? Why are we speaking sign language now?"

"Because E is for," she gestured to the whole room, "everybody can get it. The mamas, the daddies, these little bad-ass kids, and you."

Duke walked over with Charlye. "Look who I found. Had to save her from being accosted by a few of the little boys," Duke explained. "These kids are bad as hell. This little girl is over there singing Meg the Stallion?"

Blake folded her arms over her chest. "A little thot in the making." She grinned at Charlye. "Hey, girl."

Charlye laughed and gave Blake a hug. "You're so wrong for that." They hugged. She looked at me. "Hi."

I hugged her. "Hey." I hadn't expected to see her there. The last couple of weeks, she'd been hanging with her mom, helping her box up Julia's things. And I knew she was leaving for Hawaii tomorrow to spread Julia's ashes.

Blake narrowed her eyes. "Whatever you do, steer clear of that Lil' Pilar and her big-ass mouth." Needless to say, my sister wasn't a "kid" person. She only liked the kids in the family.

"Damn, baby sis," I said. "She can't be more than eight. Show her a little grace."

"I'll show *her* grace, but let me catch her mom outside. And her whack-ass daddy."

I finally greeted Duke with a dap. "What's good, bruh?"

"Shit, this barbecue. I swear, Mom thinks she's slick,

using Naija's birthday as an excuse to get me to grill. What one or two-year-old wants ribs?"

Blake and I raised our hands and shrugged. When Bliss and my mother were discussing the menu, we'd all decided that the party would be better with Duke's famous barbecue ribs and special sauce.

"I'm not two, but I want those ribs," Blake added. "Just sayin'."

Charlye's mouth curved into a smile, and she hunched a shoulder. "Me too."

"Fuck y'all." He chuckled. "Got me freezing my ass off in the middle of January."

Dallas and Preston arrived a short while later. Once again, all of us were in attendance *except* Tristan. And no one knew if he was coming. I didn't even think any of us had heard from him at all. He typically kept in touch with our parents, but I'd overheard Mom telling Dad that she hadn't talked to him in weeks.

Dallas approached us and my dad blocked her way. "Hold up." He held up his phone. "I have to snap this picture of my beautiful baby girl."

Grinning, Dallas said, "Thanks, Daddy." She brushed her hand over her hair and posed.

"I want you to remember this day," Dad continued. "It's the first day that we could *see* a baby bump."

We all dissolved into laughter. Even Preston couldn't hold it in. Dallas had been acting more pregnant than she was since the moment she'd found out she was expecting. She'd even started waddling for no apparent reason, rubbing her stomach like it was poking out, eating everything in sight. She'd even complained of back pain. It had been a running joke between us, and we'd all taken bets on when she would actually *look* pregnant.

"I think your mother won this one," Dad told us. "Go check the calendar."

Dallas gaped at him. "You bet on me? That's fu… messed up."

Dad shrugged. "Hey, we had to do something."

"You were getting on our nerves," Mom explained, rubbing Dallas' growing belly. "It's all in fun, babe."

Paityn walked over. "What did I miss?" She glanced at Dallas. "Shit, I didn't win."

Dallas glared at her. "Really, Sissy? You too?"

Clearing her throat, Paityn changed the subject, "Duke, Bliss wants to know when we can eat."

Dallas grumbled another curse, "Y'all are lucky I'm hungry. By the way…" She pulled out a pink Post-it and slapped it on my dad's chest. She stuck another on Duke's shoulder, then Blake's hand, Paityn's stomach, my forehead, and finally Mom's heart. "You're having a granddaughter. Gender reveal."

My mother's eyes widened. "Another girl? I'm so happy."

"Yeah, yeah." Dallas waved a dismissive hand. "I don't have time for pink confetti or pink powder or balloons. So, a Post-it will have to do."

Mom did a little dance and clapped. She hugged Dallas. "Preston!" She embraced my future brother-in-law and cupped his cheeks. "I'm so happy for you both."

Dad congratulated Preston and wrapped his arms around Dallas. "My baby girl is giving me a granddaughter."

"I sure am," Dallas said. "I'll expect you both to babysit and…" Then, the tears came. I'd never seen my stoic sister cry as much as I had since she announced her pregnancy to us on Halloween, our birthday. "Mom, I need you to do her hair because I suck. And, Dad, I want you to teach her everything she needs to know about life."

Preston grinned. "What about me?"

Dallas kissed her boyfriend. "You too."

We all followed suit, offering congrats and giving hugs. Soon, food was served. To escape the den of children, and since Charlye was hanging out with my sisters, I went down to the basement with my plate. When I got down there, Asa was smashing a full plate of food.

"What's up, big bruh." He picked up another rib and bit into it. "This muthafucka is good as hell."

"I bet." I joined him at the bar. My parents had made sure their house would always be a place we could gather. The finished basement was my spot. Before I'd moved out, my bedroom was down here. Ideal for the privacy I'd craved. It felt like my own apartment and had everything I needed—a kitchen, a big screen television, a sectional, a pool table, a full bathroom, and a bed.

We ate in silence for a few minutes, before Asa said, "Good to see Charlye."

I paused, rib in midair. "Yeah."

"You've been spending a lot of time over Maya's house lately."

Julia's death had been hard on her entire family. On the day she passed away, Charlye had come to me. At the time, she was inconsolable, worried for her mother, and concerned about her siblings who hadn't made it in time to say their goodbyes. I'd done the only thing I could. Be there for her, hold her, comfort her. She'd slept in my bed that night—without me.

On the day of the funeral, she'd kissed me. I'd like to believe I would've stopped it before we made love in Julia's room, but I knew I would've been helpless to stop whatever was happening between us. I'd grown accustomed to her being near me, but realistically, she lived in another state. I'd done long distance relationships before, and I was at a point in my life where I wanted proximity with the woman I shared my life with.

We'd yet to speak about what happened in Atlanta or her mother's house, but I was sure that conversation would happen sooner than later. I knew what I wanted. *Did she*? The physical attraction was there, definitely. Yet, I was well aware that she'd had a very recent breakup and lost one of the most important people in her life. All in a matter of weeks. Which gave me pause. While I was willing to throw my cards on the table after she dumped Kelvin, now I was concerned the timing wasn't right anymore. After everything she'd been through, if she were a client, I would've counseled *against* the "get over the one you were with by getting under the next one" mentality. Since I've always had her best interests at heart, no matter how I felt, that would include me.

"There's a lot of history between you two," Asa said, almost as if he'd read my mind. "A lot to consider if you decide to change the dynamics of your relationship." He leaned back in his chair and burped. "But shit... How many times do you get to be with the woman you've been feeling since you were kids?"

I eyed my brother. The youngest of the group, but in some ways, the smartest. Asa had carved out his own path, bucking family tradition in every way. Like Duke, he'd done the absolute opposite of what everyone thought he'd do. Instead of going to college right out of high school, he'd taken a gap year and traveled. That year turned into three years of seeing the world, visiting places I'd never even considered. After his twenty-first birthday, he'd enrolled at University of Michigan and earned a degree in Exercise Science. He'd followed that up with a Master of

Business Administration. Today, he owned and operated a boutique gym in Ann Arbor and still traveled as often as he could.

He chuckled. "If it were me, I'd risk it all just to see where it would end." He glanced at me and shrugged. "If you even care what I think."

Hard to believe I was staring at the same person who'd bugged the hell out of me when he was little. Asa had been a snitch, a terror who stole money from my drawer, wore my clothes when I went away to college, and told one of my girlfriends that I was getting ready to break up with her. It was true, but still… "So now that you're pushing thirty, you think I want to hear advice from you?" I teased.

"I know a little something, big bruh." He smirked. "A lot of tricks of the trade. I've seen a lot of things, met a lot of different people. Mostly I learned from y'all." He rubbed the back of his neck. "But I'm not about to get all sappy with you. Shit, I just came down here to eat without having to protect my plate from those strange kids upstairs."

I barked out a laugh. "Tell me about it."

Duke entered the area. "Man, I had to fight this little girl for the last rib." He sat next to me. "I gave her twenty dollars."

Asa cracked up. "She's gonna be rich one day. Watch."

A few minutes later, Charlye came down. She smiled. "There you are."

I swiveled in the chair. "What's up?"

"I'm going to head back to the house. I don't feel right leaving Mom there for too long by herself."

"How is she?" Duke asked.

She smiled sadly. "Hanging in there."

"Maybe I'll come by and make her dinner."

Charlye leaned against the breakfast bar. "Brunch would be better. She loves Belgian waffles."

Duke smirked. "*She* does? Or you?"

She raised her hands up. "You got me. I do."

"I got you." He winked.

I wanted to kick him off his chair. Clearing my throat, I said, "I'll walk you out."

Charlye said her goodbyes to everyone in the house and we made our way to her car. I opened the driver's door for her, but she made no move to get in. "Actually, can we talk?"

I closed the door. "Sure. You okay?"

She nodded. "Yeah." She pointed toward the back of the house. "It's cold. Can we go to your mom's she shed?"

My father had built the shed for Mom's birthday a couple of years ago. He'd spared no expense to make it into her own private oasis on the property. Inside, there was a couch that pulled out to a bed, an armchair, a table, several bookcases, a small television, a mini fridge, and a Keurig. Outside the structure, he'd even built her a patio so she could sit outside in the summer.

"I love it in here," Charlye said, taking a seat on the couch. "I want one when I grow up." She giggled. "Maybe my husband will be as generous as Papa Stew."

"She is spoiled." I sat next to her. "But she deserves it."

Charlye entwined her fingers with mine. "She does. I can't thank her enough for everything she's done for Mom, for us."

"How are you holding up?"

"Fine, I guess. Just sad."

"Ready for your trip?"

"All packed. We're meeting Elise and Justus in Cali, then we'll all take the same plane to Hawaii. Harper is already there." She swallowed visibly. "I was going crazy in the house. That's why I came today. To get out. I'm so glad I did, because y'all are a trip." She laughed. It was light, airy. Exactly what I wanted to hear. "Man, I needed to laugh. You missed it. Blake chased that little girl Pilar out of the kitchen." Charlye fell back against the cushion as a fit of giggles took over. "You should've seen that girl run. She was darting through people, dodging Blake." She smacked her legs. "Bliss had to block Blake from snatching the baby up."

I imagined my sister trying to catch Pilar. I chuckled. "She's silly."

"Your mother sent her to her room." She cracked up again. "Hilarious." She told another story about how Duke played a game of tug-of-war with a little boy who tried to take his Apple Watch. My brother had set it down so he could clean his hands and somehow the boy picked it up. "Then, Dallas started crying because the ketchup squirted on her brand-new blouse. Preston had to take her to another room. I'm telling you… I needed today."

"I'm glad my family's antics were entertaining for you."

"I love your family." She beamed. "They're my family too."

"You know they love you."

"Yeah. Makes me feel special." She sighed. "I wanted to talk to you because we haven't really talked since the funeral." She glanced at me out of the corner of her eye. "Is there a reason for that?"

"A couple of reasons," I admitted. "Work. I met with my editor about my book, developed a guest segment for Blake and Bliss' podcast. And… I figured you all needed some time to just be with each other."

She nodded. "That makes sense. I just want to be sure there was no other reason."

"No."

"Mom asked me when I was going back to Atlanta this morning."

"What did you tell her?"

"My plan is to come back here after Hawaii, but she keeps telling me she wants me to get back to my life." She linked our fingers again. "Until now, I thought I'd always live in Atlanta. My job is there, my siblings, my friends… But I'm not sure my life is there. Does that make sense?"

"It does. Do you *want* to stay?"

"In some ways. I've been spending time with Mom, you…" She closed her eyes shut and shook her head. "I'm getting to know Mom in a different way. And my father? We've talked almost every day since the funeral. I finally told him about Kelvin." She looked at me, a soft smile on her lips. "He was livid, threatened to 'crack his skull'." Her fingers held up a quote sign.

"That would be something to see."

"Pretty much."

Charlye was a pro at beating around the bush. I could listen to her talk in circles every day, but I also wanted to watch my niece eat her cake. "Char?"

She blinked. "Yeah."

"Did you want to ask me something?"

Dropping her head, she swiped her thumb over mine. It took a moment, but she lifted her eyes, held my gaze. "It's not just my parents," she admitted. "It's you. You're one of the reasons I want to stay."

I leaned into her, bumping my shoulder with hers. "That's nice to hear."

"Something's happening between us. Something new. Something exciting? Something scary," she added under her breath. Her tongue darted out to moisten her bottom lip. I followed the motion like a hawk would its prey. "I like it."

Just hearing her say that… *Damn*. Simple words, but full of sincere emotion. I'd never felt this way before, like I would do anything—beg, borrow, and steal—to hold on to the feeling. To her.

"Can we explore this?" she asked softly.

"Is that what you want?"

"Yes," she whispered. "But this isn't just about what *I* want. You spend so much time making sure everyone else has what they need. I recognize it because we're alike in that way. But I need to know… What do *you* want?"

The part of me that recognized that we might not be ready for this had been drowned out by the part of me that wanted to see where this could lead. I'd never been the type to rush into anything, but I couldn't stop myself from wanting to push past the doubt and move forward full steam ahead. I rested my forehead against hers. "You," I murmured against her mouth before I kissed her.

I lost myself in her scent, in her soft moans, in the feel of her body. She'd awakened parts of me I didn't know existed. I wanted to drop to my knees and worship her. I wanted to strip her bare, take my time with her. But I didn't want to be in my mother's she shed when we made love for the first time.

I groaned and pulled back, raking my gaze over her face. Her eyes were still closed, her mouth was swollen from our kiss, and the high ponytail she'd come to the party with was now hanging low. "Char?"

She stared at me through hooded eyes. "Yes?" she breathed.

"As much as I want this, we're in my mother's she shed."

"Right."

Standing, I pulled her to her feet. "Let's table this for a more private place."

She pouted. "Okay."

I ran my thumb over the slight frown that had formed on her brow, then brushed my lips over hers again. "We have time."

She nibbled on her bottom lip. "So what happens now?"

"Whatever you want to happen?"

Charlye quirked a brow. "Another orgasm? This time for both of us?"

I rubbed my nose against hers. "Multiple orgasms." I kissed her. "Soon."

She wrapped her arms around my neck and smiled. And I felt like she'd bathed me in sunlight. She was so beautiful, so perfect. "I'm looking forward to it," she said.

I walked her back to her car, opened the door for her. "Text me when you get home."

She agreed. "Eat lots of cake. And send me pics of Naija covered in frosting."

Laughing, I agreed to take a video. When she was safely in the car and buckled in, I shut the door. As she drove away, I thought about everything that had happened in the she shed.

Experience told me to stop, to take a moment, to create some distance between us. But my heart… Years of desire had rendered me incapable of making a decision *not* clouded by my own feelings. And, for once, I wasn't going to question it. I wanted to risk it all.

Chapter Eight

YOU'RE THE SWEETEST ONE

Charlye

"*I* think this is the last one." Mom walked into the kitchen carrying another floral arrangement, a bouquet full of pink snapdragons, lilies, hydrangea, and roses. The flowers had been arriving throughout the morning and into the afternoon, before our walk, during breakfast, while we were out running errands, and after lunch. They were everywhere, on the kitchen island, on the table, on the counter, in the living room.

I leaned in and inhaled the sweet fragrance. "Smells so good." I opened the card.

"What does it say?" Mom asked, a wide grin on her face.

"*Because you're everything,*" I read, clutching the small piece of paper to my chest.

Each note that had accompanied the flowers had a message that filled me to the brim with excitement. *Because you're worth it. Because your smile is like the Sun. Because you're intelligent. Because you deserve it. Because you're my favorite. Because you're a survivor. Because you're always on my mind. Because you're beautiful.* I tucked the latest card away in the small box where I'd kept the others. I wanted to save them, I wanted to remember this day for the rest of my life.

Mom ran her finger over a pink rose. "Who do you think they're from?"

I pulled out the rose and handed it to her. My heart wanted them to be from Dex, but I wasn't sure. Although he was in Florida for business, he could've executed all this online. Yet, we'd talked several times today, via text, on the phone. We'd even video chatted for a couple of minutes during lunch. He hadn't mentioned it.

After Naija's birthday party, Dex had made it very clear that he wanted to do this the right way. And I loved that he was sorta old-fashioned in that he wanted to date me. Yet, the business of life had prevented us from going out.

Mom and I just returned from Atlanta last night. While we were in Hawaii, we'd decided to fly back with my siblings. The spur-of-the-moment trip worked because it gave me a chance to handle some business, grab more clothes, and talk to my boss about extending my leave. My mother just wanted to spend more time with my siblings and Ellis. Now that Julia was gone, she'd admitted that she felt a little useless, like she had nothing to do.

"The better question," Mom said, "is who do you *want* them to be from?" I looked up in time to catch the smirk on my mother's face and it dawned on me that she'd been playing me.

"Mom!" I laughed. "This whole time you've known, and you've been acting like you didn't?"

The coy smile on her lips confirmed everything I already knew. She shrugged. "I've been sworn to secrecy."

"Why can't you tell me who it is?"

"It's not my news to tell, sweetie."

I narrowed my eyes. "So, what is your role in this exactly? Are you reporting back all of my reactions or something?"

She burst out in a fit of giggles. "No. I'm just here to give my stamp of approval. And because I love to see you smile."

I hugged my mother. "I love you."

Mom placed a kiss to my forehead. Leaning back, she met my gaze. I noticed the tears swimming in her eyes immediately. "You've been such a blessing to me. From the moment I saw your beautiful face, you've brought me nothing but joy. I've watched you put yourself last to support the people you love. I've watched you struggle to find the value in yourself that we already know is there. I've watched you excel in a male-dominated field. I've watched you work through unimaginable odds to carve out a life for yourself. You are everything that those cards said and more. You should be proud of the woman you've become because I am. I love you. I want you to embrace happiness."

With one speech, my mother had spoken to the ten-year-old me who felt unpretty, unwanted, unloved. She'd just encouraged the fourteen-year-old me who felt so lonely, so alone. All my life I'd struggled with my self-image, with my self-worth. For so long, I saw the beauty in everyone around me, but couldn't find it in myself. Even though I had an awesome family, a mother who championed me, siblings who protected me, I still didn't quite feel like I belonged. Listening to my mother's words, remembering my last conversation with Julia, hearing Dex say he was proud of me... I'd never felt so loved. And I *wanted* to embrace it.

My chin trembled. "Mom, you're not supposed to make me cry. Not with all these beautiful flowers here."

She brushed my cheeks, wiping away the evidence. "You're not crying. It's the onion we just cut up."

I chuckled. "Right."

Mom kissed my brow again. "You need to get yourself together, though. You have another surprise coming."

I frowned. "What surprise? What do you know?"

"I know that you have plans for the afternoon. Get dressed."

I stood there, staring at my mom as she shifted a vase to another spot on the island and finished cutting the onion for the fried potatoes she'd decided to cook for an afternoon snack.

She lifted her eyes and arched a brow. "Yes?" I opened my mouth to speak, but nothing came out. "Sweetie?"

"I... um." I pointed toward the hallway. "I'm just gonna go upstairs and get dressed."

"That's my girl. Go on now." As I walked up the stairs, my mind running in all directions, I heard my mom call after me, "Pack an overnight bag."

I paused and headed back downstairs. "Can you give me a little more? A hint on how I should dress?"

"For now, just something comfortable," she told me. "Don't forget your lip gloss."

I spent at least twenty minutes in front of the closet, staring at my limited wardrobe options. Under normal situations, not knowing details would have stressed me the fuck out. But all I felt was giddy excitement at what's to come. Finally, I settled on a knitted lounge set I'd recently purchased online. It took a little while longer to pack a bag because I had no idea where I was going.

Ultimately, I decided on jeans and a sweater. My go-to look.

When I'd finally finished, I carried my bag downstairs. Mom had already started frying the potatoes. It smelled like heaven doused in sautéed onions and garlic. "I'm all…" I gasped.

In the center of the island was a new bouquet of flowers, this one filled with lavender roses, purple and green orchids, and green mums mixed with calathea leaves, lily grass and other greens. *So beautiful.*

"It's gorgeous, isn't it?" Mom said.

"It is." I approached the island and studied the bouquet. "I can't believe it." When I spotted the card, I pulled it out and opened it.

Because you check all of my boxes, allow me to appreciate you.
See you soon, Pretty.
Dex

"What did this one say?" Mom asked, stirring the potatoes. "Did he finally reveal himself?" I handed her the card. She flashed a wide grin. "I knew that boy was good for you."

"When did Dex tell you he was going to do this?"

Ignoring my question, she asked, "When did you and Dex decide to give this a shot? Last I knew, you were just friends."

I gave my mother the short version minus the orgasm and the mini make-out session in her house. "I don't know… I like the way I am with him. He's awakened emotions in me that were dormant, that I didn't know I could feel." I stared at the flowers. "I just realized I wanted to hold on to that."

"That's so beautiful, sweetie. But you're not done." She set a card on the counter in front of me.

I picked it up and flipped it over. My name was written

across the front in beautiful calligraphy. "I almost don't want to open it."

"You probably should."

I opened the envelope and pulled out the card. It read: *Because I want to pamper you.*

Inside, was another blank envelope. I eyed my mother as I ripped it open. "Oh my God." It was a gift certificate to IMMERSE Spa at the MGM Grand Casino in Detroit. "He bought me a spa day!"

"Your driver is outside. Your first appointment is at three o'clock."

"Driver?" I walked to the window. Sure enough, there was a dark SUV waiting in the driveway. "This is crazy! It's too much."

"It's called pamper for a reason, dear." She brought my bag over to me and steered me toward the front door. "You'll stay overnight. The suite is already paid for, and the details are in this card." She gave me yet another envelope. "And I'll see you in the morning." She kissed my cheek. "Love you."

When I got in the SUV, I sent Dex a text: *I don't know what to say. Thank you.*

It only took a second for his response to come through: *Just wait… Enjoy the spa.*

The forty-minute ride to Detroit was quiet, but my thoughts were loud. As good as it felt to be spoiled, the thought of him doing all of this for me made me slightly uncomfortable. And experience had shown me that shit like this always came with a price. Besides, I was used to doing everything myself, paying for my own massages and waxes, driving my own car to appointments and on errands. I was extremely budget-conscious. I rarely splurged on overnight trips or room service. But I would try to enjoy the incredible gift, if only because *Dex* had given it to me.

My first appointment was a deep-body massage, followed by a HydraFacial treatment, and ending with the signature manicure and pedicure. For dinner, Dex had ordered room service and I fell asleep while we video chatted. The next morning, the same black SUV picked me up and drove me home.

The smell of vanilla, cinnamon, and bacon permeated the air when I walked in the door. I dropped my overnight bag and headed to the kitchen.

"Good morning." Duke stood at the stove, slicing strawberries. "You're right on time."

I approached him. "What are you…? You're cooking for me?"

"Have a seat," he said. "There's something for you on the table."

A box with a big red bow sat atop the table. I picked it up. *Heavy.* I glanced back at Duke to find him watching me with interest.

He smirked. "Hurry your slow ass up, Char. You got shit to do today."

I set the box back down, pulled the ribbon off, and lifted the lid. "Oh my God!" I shouted, pulling out the brand-new leather electrician tool set. I wrapped the belt around my waist. "How…? I've been wanting this for so long." The card in the box read: *Because you needed it.*

I thought back to a conversation I'd had with Justus about my current tool belt. He'd clowned me because it was basically falling apart and had even offered to purchase another one. Of course, I'd turned him down, but I remembered showing him this one. I'd promised myself that I would buy it as soon as the wedding was over, but then…

Dex was Justus' best friend. That simple fact alone was a very good reason to tread lightly with Dex. I never wanted to do anything that would put a strain on *their* relationship. Knowing that Dex had consulted Justus about this gift warmed my heart. Because it meant that my brother had given his blessing to whatever was unfolding between us.

The urge to call my brother prompted me to grab my phone out of my purse, but before I could call him, Duke set a full plate in front of me.

"Eat," he ordered, sliding yet another card over to me.

This one said: *Because I listen.*

A discussion at Naija's birthday party came to mind. I'd mentioned something about Duke cooking for me. And Dex had made it happen. Breakfast consisted of Belgian waffles with whipped cream and fresh berries, crispy bacon, scrambled eggs with lots of cheese, and freshly squeezed orange juice. All my favorites.

Mom breezed into the kitchen, a big smile on her face. "There you are." She kissed me and took her seat at the corner nook. Duke brought her a plate as well. "Yum. Thank you, baby."

While we ate, I filled Mom in on the spa experience and the latest gift. By the time we'd finished eating, Duke had disappeared, leaving us with a clean kitchen and a chicken lasagna in the oven for Mom.

The doorbell interrupted our conversation about the television show Mom had binged last night. I stacked the plates and took them to the dishwasher, while she answered the door. My mother returned with Mama V.

I hugged her. "What a surprise!"

Mama V leaned on the island and took a few deep breaths. "Shoot, I'm out of breath. That's what I get for eating two of Duke's cinnamon rolls. My son is so damn talented in that kitchen."

I giggled. "He made us waffles this morning."

Mama V winked. "I know." She rounded the island and gently took the plate from me. "I can do that."

"Oh no, Mama V. I don't want you to wash the dishes. You can relax with Mom." We played a little tug-of-war with a plate, until she gave me *that* look, the one that every kid knew not to test. I finally let go and held up my hands. "Yes, ma'am."

Mama V flashed a wide smile. "That's what I thought." She finished the dishes in silence while Mom chatted with her about something I knew nothing about. "Charlye, I don't want you to worry about your mother while you're gone. That's why I'm here."

I blinked. "What?"

Mama V handed me a card. "No buts, chile."

My mouth fell open when I realized the envelope contained a flight itinerary. My heart stammered in my chest as I scanned the flight information, the destination, the times. And my eyes filled with tears when I read the message: *Because I want to date you. In person. Counting the minutes.*

Dex had really outdone himself. Every gift, every note… I felt overwhelmed yet excited, nervous but happy. I braced myself against the counter and took several cleansing breaths. Scanning the room, I thought about everything, took in the evidence of Dex's affection. Flowers. Notes. My new tool belt. He'd treated me to a spa day, he'd hired his brother to make me waffles. He'd done everything I'd hoped Kelvin would've done throughout our years-long relationship. He'd put every man I'd ever dated to shame in one day, with one perfect kiss, with one hot orgasm. Yet, some small part still couldn't believe that it was all for me.

I felt my mother's hand on my back. "Sweetie? Are you okay?"

I opened my mouth to speak but closed it because I didn't know what to say.

"Char?" Mama V called, feeling my forehead. It was a *her* thing. "Maybe she ate too many waffles?"

Mom chuckled. "I think she's just in shock."

"Maybe?" Mama V tilted her head and met my gaze. "Sweetie, I get it. It's overwhelming to say the least. Especially if you're not used to being the center of attention."

I nodded. "I…"

Mama V cupped my cheek. "And that's fine. I can see that you're scared, but don't let fear keep you from him. If you want to be with Dex, go to him."

"She's right," Mom agreed. "It's time to make a decision. Miami or nah?"

I laughed. My mom and Mama V had taken trying to keep up with the latest sayings to another level. "Thank you," I said. "I guess I have a plane to catch. I love you both."

"Love you too," Mama V said. "Now, you might want to go pack. Your flight leaves very soon."

Even as I'd resolved to take the next step, my feet were seemingly glued to the floor. I couldn't move. Mom squeezed my shoulders and turned me toward the staircase, whispering, "Char, you have to move to pack. Go." She plucked the envelope out of my hand. "I'll print your boarding pass."

It didn't take long for me to pack, probably because my mother and Mama V had taken it upon themselves to hurry my ass along. Once everything was loaded in the Uber, I settled in the back seat for the drive to Detroit

Metro Airport. Before we arrived at the McNamara Terminal, my phone buzzed. I smiled and accepted the video chat request. "Hey, sis."

Elise grinned. "Are you at the airport yet?"

I looked out the window. "Almost."

"You better enjoy every minute of the trip."

"I can't believe you didn't tell me this was going down."

"Then it wouldn't have been a surprise. But since I know you, I figured I'd call and give you a little pep talk."

I frowned. "For what?"

"Sis, stop questioning it and enjoy the ride. Let him spoil you. You deserve it."

I nibbled on my bottom lip. "But he's doing all this… I'm different in a relationship than I am as a friend. Expectations aren't the same. What if we don't click like that? What if we don't have anything to talk about?" I eyed the driver and whispered, "What if we're not compatible in the bedroom? What if—?"

"Char, stop. It's Dex. You two are perfectly content talking about everything and nothing. The chemistry is already there. He hasn't changed, neither have you. You'll be fine."

"This feels like a dream."

"Because it is. I hate seeing you like this, doubting yourself."

For some reason, I couldn't shake that niggling feeling in the back of my mind that this wasn't real, that I wasn't the right woman for him. "He could have anybody." My voice sounded small to my own ears.

"He wants *you*," she countered. Her eyes softened. "I wish you could see how dope you really are."

"I'm getting better," I said lamely.

"Keep working at it."

The car stopped. "Well, I'm here. I'll call you later."

She grinned. "Have fun. But don't come back pregnant."

I swiped the call off and thanked the driver. Elise was right. It was just Dex. I'd known him since we were kids. He gave his Superman ice cream to me when the mean kids took mine. He'd threatened to hurt every boy who bullied me in school. He lent me his shoulder to cry on several times for various reasons. In all the years I'd known him, he had never let me down. Dex had already shown me through his actions that he thought I was worthy to be treasured. It was my turn to trust that, to not assume the worst, to enjoy the moment. To enjoy *him*. And that's exactly what I planned to do.

Chapter Nine

READY OR NOT

Dexter

"*L*adies, I have a special guest today. You've been asking for that all-too-valuable relationship advice and I have a treat for you. One of my fave people in the world is here. Dexter Young, Relationship Expert. Welcome, Dex."

I smiled at radio show host, Deja Taylor. "What's up, D? Thanks for having me."

Deja was a host of a popular morning show podcast geared toward black women. Her and her crew had made a name for themselves by offering a variety of content from entertainment news to sports commentary to political content. One of their most popular segments was the book club segment. After she'd read my book, she contacted me and asked me to be her guest.

"Ladies, let me tell you…" she said, "…this man is

117

giving off that Big Big Energy. Clean than-a-mug. Classic. Fine as all else."

I smirked at my friend. "Really?"

Deja arched a brow. "You know I call it how I see it. Ladies, Dex and I have known each other for years. He recently published his debut book, *It's not the Hookup, It's the Chase*. And I'm so grateful that he stopped by."

"I'm glad to be here."

"Whew, ladies." She smacked the table and let out an exaggerated sigh. "That voice!"

Deja launched into the story of how we met. We'd attended Hampton University together. From the moment we'd met, we were tight. We both majored in Psychology, enjoyed photography, and ran track. We'd even dated for a minute—until we realized that we were better as friends. Which was a good thing because she was now happily married with one child on the way.

"But trust me," she continued, "He's one of the best men I know, doing good work out here."

I laughed. "Thank you."

We spent the bulk of the show talking about the book, about my job as a professional wingman and relationship coach, and a little about my personal life. It wasn't the first time I'd done a radio show, but it was the *only* time I'd enjoyed it. Probably because I was talking to a friend.

"So, I wanted to do something different today," she suggested. "I'm going to let you all ask Coach Dex those burning questions you have about your current bae, your potential bae, and your love lives." Deja gave out the call-in number. Several seconds later, the phone lines lit up with callers. She turned off the mic, a wide grin on her face. "See, I told you."

When we talked on the phone, she'd promised me their listeners would be all over this segment. She wasn't wrong.

The questions ranged from specific to broad, from simple to complex. The more they came, the more I realized Duke might have been on to something regarding my own show.

Caller number seven was the first guy that had called. "Yo, I was wondering... How can I get more hoes?"

Deja hung up. "What we're not gon' do is entertain that bull—" a loud horn drowned out the *shit*. "If you call with something reckless, you will get the dial tone."

The next caller in the queue introduced herself as Dawn. "Hi, Coach Dex."

"Hello," I replied.

"I was just wondering if you were single. Asking for a friend."

Before I could answer, Deja shook her head and pointed at the mixer on the other side of the glass and a clip of Ginuwine's song "None of Ur Friends Business" played over the speaker.

Jasmine was caller nine. She asked a sincere question about her current relationship of ten years. After she'd dissolved into tears on air, I consoled her for a moment. "I think it's safe to say that your man isn't the one for you. Maybe it's time to re-examine what you want in a partner, but first you should take a hard look at yourself. It's okay to take some time before you get into another relationship. No need to rush."

My own words taunted me, made me feel like a hypocrite in several ways. Essentially, I'd given this woman the same advice I *should've* given Char. Yet, my own desire for her had prompted a different response.

Charlye was currently in the air, on her way to me. I couldn't discount the facts, though. I absolutely planned to spend all weekend romancing her, spoiling her, showing her how much I wanted her. Because she deserved it. And because I...loved her. Would I tell her that? *No*. For me, it was just a simple fact of my life, a part of me that had existed since we were kids. She could take it or leave it, but it didn't make it any less true. Still, that caller had me questioning myself. *Am I doing the right thing?*

"You okay?" Deja asked.

I nodded. "I'm good."

"One more call?"

"Sure."

The last caller, Diamond, spoke candidly about her lack of attraction for her current man. The conversation was going okay until she declared, "I just want to have your babies."

I met Deja's eyes and we both laughed. "Thanks, Diamond," I said. "But I agree with you that sexual attraction is important in any relationship. Ask yourself if you can stay with someone who doesn't fulfill that need. Based off your response to me, I suspect your answer is no. In that case, it's probably time to call it quits."

Deja agreed. "And girl... Take several seats. Telling a stranger you want to have their kids? I mean, he's fine and all, but damn." A few minutes later, Deja closed the show. "If you haven't read Dex's book, go ahead and grab your copy. If you're lucky, you'll be able to catch Dex on one of the many stops on his upcoming book tour. Byyyeeee!"

"Thank you," I told her once the mics were off. "That was..."

"A trip!" Deja stood and hugged me. "You did great, though. Are you sure you don't want to have your own show?"

Admittedly, I hadn't been too keen on radio. But I wouldn't rule it out anymore. "Not right now."

"Well, I want to have you back on."

"Anytime."

She tilted her head, assessing me quietly. "I don't know what's going on, but I'm going to guess that it's about a woman."

I frowned. "Why would you say that?"

"Something got to you while you were taking calls. One of the callers. Jasmine?"

I dropped my head. "Nothing gets past you." It never had. Deja noticed everything, especially things she shouldn't. "But I'm good."

"You never share."

"What?"

She grinned. "I've known you for several years and there is always a part of you that seems inaccessible. I know you have a big family, but I wonder if *they* even know."

"Know what?"

"The parts of you that you're intent to hide."

I chuckled. "My family is full of therapists of all types and Duke. Trust me, they see. And they call me out every chance they get."

She squeezed my arm. "Good. I'm glad you have an outlet. How long are you in town?"

"I decided to stay through the weekend."

She arched a brow. "Oh, so are you staying with a woman?"

"Why do you care?"

Deja giggled. "Okay, okay. I might be trying to play matchmaker. Chaz' sister is such a beautiful person. She needs a good guy. And I think you'd like her."

"Even if I was interested, I couldn't let *you* hook me up."

She gaped at me. "Why?"

While I knew that several successful marriages had started as the result of a former girlfriend or boyfriend playing matchmaker, I stayed away from friends of my exes. Too much potential drama. "You know why?"

She pouted. "That was ages ago. Despite what I said on the radio show, I'm happy with Chaz. You know that."

"Let's keep it that way," I said. "I better get out of here. I have to head to the airport."

Deja's brows lowered in confusion. "I thought you were staying the weekend."

"I almost forgot you were nosy as hell."

"Oh, shut up. Just admit I'm right then."

"Admit what, D?"

"There is someone."

I was tempted to talk to Deja, to gain another woman's perspective outside of my sisters. Yet, I hesitated, because the only person I needed to talk to about Char was... *Char*. "Maybe." I hugged Deja and walked to the door. "Thanks again, D. I'll talk to you soon. Tell Chaz I said what's up."

Traffic going to the airport was light, and I arrived early. Once I parked, I dialed my mother since she'd left several messages.

"Hey, babe," Mom chirped. "How are you?"

"I'm good, Ma."

"Did Charlye make it in yet?"

I glanced at my watch. Char's flight wasn't due to land for another ten minutes. "Not yet."

My mother initiated a video chat and I accepted. "I just needed to see your face."

I smiled but didn't speak.

Mom stared at me, her eyes seeing everything I couldn't say out loud. "You've outdone yourself, son. Charlye was so happy."

I closed my eyes as more doubts filled the empty spaces of my mind. "That's good."

"Sometimes we can think so much about a decision

that we talk ourselves out of it." She flashed a sad smile, but she forged ahead, "You're doubting yourself. I could always tell, even when you thought you were hiding it from me. But what I've come to realize, what all of us know… You're the counselor, the most like your father in that aspect."

"I thought that was Duke," I grumbled.

"Duke is good, but his gift is not yours. I've watched you all your life. You're the backbone for your sisters and brothers. When they need someone to inspire, to lift spirits, to encourage, to hold them up, to guide, they call you. You're logical, so methodical in your approach that you don't allow for your own feelings. As a result, when you do decide to follow your heart, it doesn't feel right to you."

I swallowed. "What if it isn't the right time for Charlye?"

"Why do you think that?"

"She just got out of a relationship, not because she wanted to, but because he cheated on her."

"And?" Mom argued. "She didn't love him."

I frowned. "Did she tell you that?"

"She didn't have to." Mom cleared her throat. "I'm quite capable of paying attention to cues myself. I taught you a thing or two."

I laughed. My mother had a way of breaking a thing down to the simplest terms.

"I know you," she continued. "You've never rushed into anything without a thought. I don't believe you would've done everything you did for her yesterday and today if you didn't consider everything."

Resting my head against the seat, I blew out a deep breath. "I want her, Ma," I admitted. "I've always wanted her. You know as well as I do that fact could've clouded my mind."

"Did you talk to Charlye?"

"I did."

"What did she say?"

"That she wanted to explore us."

"Okay, then."

"*After* I stayed with her, *after* I supported her, *after* I helped her in every way I could. Julia's death was hard on her and the family. And I was there."

Mom chuckled. "You've always been there. What makes this time different?"

I grumbled a curse. I didn't have a good argument against my mother's logic. So I didn't even try to argue. "I don't know."

"Dex, trust Charlye to know what she wants. Most importantly, trust yourself. Don't talk yourself out of being happy with the woman you love. Now, you better get going. No son of mine should ever let their lady carry her own luggage."

The corners of my mouth tugged upward. "I know what to do, Ma."

"I know you do, son. I love you. Have fun."

When I ended the call, I made my way to baggage claim. Several minutes passed before I spotted Charlye descending on the escalator, so beautiful in dark ripped jeans and a simple white t-shirt. I made my way toward the escalator.

When she finally noticed me, she smiled. "Dex." She approached me. "Hi."

"Hi." I stared into her eyes, torn between pulling her closer and pushing her away. "How was your flight?"

She beamed up at me. "Good."

We stood there for a moment, looking at each other. Awkward and unsure had never been us. But that's exactly how it felt. Well, how *I* felt.

"Maybe we…"

"I think we…"

Charlye laughed nervously and gestured toward me. "Sorry. I had so many things I wanted to say when I saw you, but… Yeah, that was super awkward."

I chuckled. "Very."

She brushed her hand over the back of her neck and nibbled on her bottom lip. "Dex, I know you probably have something big planned, but I'm wondering if we can just spend some alone time together."

I could take that several ways. I knew what immediately flashed through my mind—her sitting on my face or my dick. But I didn't want to assume that was *her* version of alone time. "Alone as in…?"

"No fancy dresses, no five-star restaurant, no polite talk. Just us." Her eyes widened as if she realized what I was asking her. "Talking," she blurted out. "Um, I want to talk."

I covered my smile with my hand and cleared my throat. "That's cool." I grabbed her carry-on and gestured toward the doors. "Ready when you are."

Chapter Ten

SOMEDAY IS TONIGHT

Dexter

"*O*MG, this is so good." Charlye bit into her sandwich.

We'd spent the afternoon on a Little Havana Food & Cultural Tour. Our latest stop was Old's Havana Cuban Bar & Cocina. We'd already sampled empanadas, learned about the art of cigar-rolling, strolled through an open-air market, and had mojitos. Now, we were eating Cubano sandwiches.

I scarfed down the rest of my food and nodded. "Mm hmm."

"I'm going to be so full. You might have to roll me to the hotel." She laughed. "Especially if I eat churros *and* ice cream."

"I think that's next."

She groaned, leaning back in her chair and patting her stomach. "I'll probably gain the twenty pounds I lost in one day." Then, she sat up and did a little happy chair dance. "But I'm going to eat anyway."

I chuckled. "That's why we're here. I know you love Cuban food."

She finished her sandwich. "I sure do."

After we left the restaurant, we headed to Domino Park. As we walked through the small park, we settled into comfortable silence. Throughout the afternoon, the awkwardness we'd experienced at the airport was gone. We were back to being Dex and Char, and it felt right.

She bumped into me and entwined our fingers. "Thank you." She rested her head against my arm. "I love everything about this."

"You're welcome."

As the group moved ahead, we trailed behind, checking out the murals, watching the men play dominoes. The next stop was Azucar Ice Cream. It took Char a few minutes to choose her flavor, Café con leche. I ordered Cuban vanilla.

We took a seat on a nearby bench. "Delicious," she mumbled, eyeing my ice cream. "Trade?" We switched cones. "Yum. I love this one too."

"I think I like yours better," I told her.

She bobbed her head. "Me too." She sighed. "I haven't been to Miami in so long. It's a lot different than I remember."

Curious, I asked, "How old were you the last time you came here?"

"It was right after I moved to Atlanta, so I was about twenty." She smiled. "I made some terrible choices back then. I was so angry, so frustrated with my life. So lost."

When Charlye moved, I'd purposely kept my distance for a while. At the time, I'd told myself I was giving her space. But I knew it was because I needed to move on, to reset my expectations, to forget about the possibility of us being together as anything more than friends. Hearing her talk like this, seeing the pain in her eyes, I realized I had no idea what she'd been through, what she'd endured. Obviously, there was a lot I didn't know about the woman sitting next to me.

She let out a humorless chuckle. "For so long, I felt like a failure, like I'd never find my way. When I came here, I met this older white man. Jack. He told me he wanted to take care of me. I never believed him, but I stayed with him for two years. No one knew about him, not even Elise. And I'd only confided in one person after I ended it. He lavished me with expensive jewelry, whisked me away to exotic locations. Then, I found out he was married, with three children who were my age. When I tried to leave him, he threatened to hurt me and my family."

Rage, hot and blinding, consumed me. "Did he...?" I didn't even notice I'd balled my hands into fists until she gripped one and squeezed.

"Jack never hit me," she explained. "He died several years ago. I found out because his attorney contacted me. He left me a little cash. I used part of it to pay for school."

"That's smart."

"After I left him, I avoided Miami because I didn't want to face the memory of him. While we were together, despite the gifts and the vacations, I never felt like he truly wanted me. He only wanted to possess me, to own me. Everything felt transactional. There was no emotion behind the attention."

Everything started to make sense, her request to avoid five-star restaurants, the fact that she wanted to keep it simple. I wondered if the gifts I'd sent had triggered memories of Jack as well. "If I'd known—"

"No." She turned to me. "Dex, the only reason I

brought that up was to tell you that this entire experience has been amazing, nothing like it was with Jack. The flowers, the notes, the gifts, your unwavering support… it was everything I didn't know I needed. Miami is different with you and I'm grateful. When I'm with you, I feel safe. When I'm with you, I feel like a better version of myself. I've always felt this way around you." She smirked. "One day, I'll tell you more about my life without you, but for now, I just want to enjoy our time together."

My mother's words filtered through my mind. *Trust Charlye to know what she wants.*

"Dex?" She searched my eyes. "I spent the entire flight ticking off the reasons we shouldn't do this."

"Honestly?"

"Of course."

"Me too," I confessed.

She eyed me quizzically. "Why?"

"You first."

She pouted. "Fine." She toyed with her necklace. "Because you're my friend. Because I feel so many things when we're together. Because those feelings make me want to run. I don't want to hurt you, and I don't want to get hurt."

"I understand that. I feel the same way, actually."

"Really?"

I lifted a brow. "Did you think I was bullshitting on those notes I sent you?"

"Good point." She ran her thumb over one of the rips in her jeans. "If we're both feeling this way, should we slow things down? Get to know each other as we are now?"

"Is that what you want?"

"I'm not answering that until you tell me what *you* want? It's your turn to go first."

"I already know who *I* want, Char." I brushed a stray

piece of hair from her face. "But we can take this as slow as you need—until you're sure."

"It's when you say things like that…" Char gripped my shirt into her palm, pulled me closer, and kissed me. "Okay, I'm sure."

"What happened to taking this slow?"

"We don't have to make any decisions today. We can talk about it later." She pressed another soft kiss to my lips. "In the morning. After you orgasm me?"

Damn. I prided myself on knowing exactly what to say or do at any given moment. Yet, the only thing I knew for sure was that I'd pretty much do anything for Charlye. I spotted the tour guide ahead and stood, pulling Char to her feet.

"Where are we going?" she asked, confusion on her face.

"It's time to go." We caught up to the group quickly. I handed the guide a fifty-dollar bill, thanked him for the tour, and led Charlye back to my rental car.

Thirty minutes later, we stumbled into my suite, mouths fused together, hands fumbling for buttons and zippers.

She tugged my shirt off. "Shit," she mumbled, scraping her nails down my stomach. "Damn, you're so… You're fine as hell."

I laughed.

She took a step back, letting her wide eyes travel from my stomach to my mouth. "I'm so serious." She giggled. "Just so you know, I'm a little nervous."

"Why?"

"Because you're going to be naked. And so am I."

"In a few short minutes."

"Right." She let out a shaky breath and turned the light off.

"We're not doing that," I told her, flicking it back on. I gripped her hips and pulled her closer. "I told you… I don't want you to hide from me."

She nodded. "Okay."

Slowly, I pulled her t-shirt off. "Because you're so beautiful."

Her eyes fluttered closed. "Dex," she whispered.

I brushed my mouth over her shoulders, over the space between her breasts. "Because I want to see you." I unhooked her bra and let it fall to the floor. "Because I want to touch you." I took one nipple into my mouth and bit down gently. "Because I want your legs wrapped around me." I lifted her in my arms and carried her over to the bed. Lowering her down, I peeled her jeans and panties off. "Because I want you." I stood over her, taking her in. There was no part of her that I didn't want to explore. I wanted her in every way. I wanted all of her—mind, body, spirit.

"Please," she begged.

I dropped to my knees and pulled her to the edge of the bed. "Because I want to taste you." I sucked her clit into my mouth. She cried out, pleading with me to keep going, to never stop. When I felt her tremble against me, I knew it wouldn't be long. "It's okay," I assured her. "Come on my tongue."

And she did. Long and hard, calling my name over and over again. She collapsed onto the mattress. A moment later, she opened her eyes. A satisfied smile formed on her lips. But I wasn't done with her yet. I needed more.

As she stared at me, I grabbed my wallet, pulled out a condom, and put it on. I licked my way up her body to her mouth. "Because I want you to remember who made you feel this way," I whispered, sinking inside her and swallowing her gasp with another kiss.

Shit. She felt so good, so warm, so tight… I closed my eyes to center myself.

She nipped my chin and wrapped her legs around my waist. "Dex," she murmured. "Please."

"Because you're everything," I grumbled against her ear, enjoying the soft moan that escaped her mouth.

I wanted to stay there forever, immersed in her, connected to her. I set the pace. Slow and easy, fast and frantic. It was the way she moaned, the way she whispered my name, the way she responded to me, the way we fit together… I couldn't get enough of her.

Charlye came first, gasping for air as she groaned my name. My own orgasm came seconds later, so hard that it felt like I was coming undone, unraveling. When I could breathe normally again, I rolled onto my back, pulling her against my side.

Seconds later, she said, "Dex?"

"Hm?" She didn't speak right away, so I leaned back, meeting her waiting gaze. "What is it?"

She smirked. "I really love going *slow* with you."

I barked out a laugh. "Just so you know," I murmured against her lips, "I definitely plan to take my time with you."

Charlye

"Get out." I laughed. "Did that really happen?

Dex nodded. "It did. Right in front of my sisters."

I covered my face. "Oh no! Who does that?"

It was our last night in Miami. We'd spent most of our

time holed up in the suite, exploring each other. In between the bedroom and wall and floor and rental car action, we'd visited the botanical gardens, went to Jungle Island, and watched *The Wiz* at Soundscape Park. It was simply perfect.

Tonight, we decided to order room service and soak in the private jacuzzi on our balcony. Dex had just finished telling me about his last failed relationship, from their first meeting to the moment she'd told him she wished she'd dated Duke.

"Apparently, she did," he murmured.

We'd spent so many years on the periphery of each other's lives, it felt good getting to know him again, listening to him talk about his experiences and his goals and even some of his fears. And I didn't mind being vulnerable around him, sharing more about my life. Even the parts I'd never told anyone else.

I leaned my head against the rim of the hot tub and closed my eyes, letting the heat of the water and the soothing bubbles lull me into a relaxed state. "Can I ask you a question?" I asked.

"Anything."

I cracked one eye open. "Have you ever cheated on one of your girlfriends?"

"No" was his answer. "That's not to say that I haven't been tempted by other women while in a relationship because I have. I just don't get down like that."

"Have you ever been cheated on?"

"Not that I know of."

I wished I could say the same thing. During my freshman year at Hampton, my very first boyfriend, Louis, admitted to fucking one of my roommates while I was in Economics class—for the entire semester. After I broke things off with Jack, I got involved with a friend of Elise's husband. Phil was nice and all, but he was also a serial cheater. Shattered my heart. Then, there was Kelvin…

"I've never cheated, but I've had my heart broken more times than I care to remember. When I went out with Kelvin," I explained, "I thought *he* was the safe choice. It wasn't a love thing; it was just comfortable. You know what happened with that."

"Char, you can't make their choices your problem."

The next question stayed on the tip of my tongue because I wasn't sure how he'd respond.

"Is that all you wanted to ask me?" he said.

I bit down on my lip, released it, and asked, "We've never talked about this before, but I want you to finally set the record straight."

His brows drew down in confusion. "Okay?"

"Why did you let me ask Logan Harris out if you knew he would turn me down?"

Dex blinked.

I broke out in a fit of giggles. "Once I realized you knew all along, I was so mad at you."

He quirked a brow. "Since we're being honest, I did know. He was a punk-ass muthafucka."

"So…?"

"It wasn't my best decision," he admitted. "Yet, I thought I was helping you by supporting what you wanted. You know we were fresh outta high school, right? I'm much wiser now."

"But you…" I blew out a slow breath. "…had feelings for me?" Our first kiss, *my* first kiss, had caught me completely off guard.

Dex pinned me with his intense stare, the one that made me feel warm and safe and…wanted. "I did."

"It's weird because, at the time, I couldn't believe that."

"Why is that?"

"Come on, Dex. You could have anybody you want—then and now. I was just Charlye. In *some* ways I'm better than I was back then. Yet, in *many* ways, I'm still the same me."

He gripped my thighs and tugged me onto his lap, wrapping my legs around his waist. "You're right. We've never had this conversation. I was wrong about a lot of things that night. Maybe I should've handled it differently, but I wasn't wrong for wanting to spend time with you, to kiss you."

"I was wrong too. I ran from you so many times. Even when I wanted to stay." I swept my thumbs over his jawline. "I'm not gonna lie, though, running is comfortable for me. I'm trying to do better at facing my life head on. Dex, this is new for me. I've never felt comfortable telling any man what I want or need."

"It's work." He brushed his finger over my chin. "We have time, though."

"Is that the lesson?"

He searched my face. "Explain?"

"*You* said we have time. *I* asked if we should slow this down. Maybe we shouldn't question it anymore? Take each moment as it comes?"

"That's hard for me."

"I know."

Dex brought my hand up to his mouth and kissed my pulse point. "But what's the alternative?"

"Nothing I want to consider."

He closed his eyes and circled my nose with his. "Good to know." He buried his face in my neck.

For some reason, I babbled on, even as my body burned with need to be closer to him, to feel him inside me. "You're so used to being in control."

He rubbed his nose over my ear, placed a soft kiss there, before he whispered, "Not with you."

Oh shit. Everything about this moment felt surreal. His lips were warm against my skin, but his whispered confession… "Dex," I breathed, when he nipped my shoulder.

"Shhh…" He licked the same spot. "Enough talking."

He gripped my chin and pulled me in for a kiss, devouring me with his mouth, his tongue, and his teeth. His dick stirred beneath me, and I rocked into it. It was embarrassing how much I wanted him. My feelings for him grew more intense by the hour, by the second. Nothing else mattered in the moment. Not my past, not my fears. Only us.

His hand slipped between my thighs and his thumb circled my clit. Once, twice, a few more times… And then I came. My orgasm buzzed through me, taking me by surprise with its intensity. I slumped forward, taking several deep breaths.

As satisfied as I felt, I wasn't ready for the night to end. I slid my hand inside his trunks and wrapped my fist around his dick. Hard. Thick. Brushing my thumb over the tip, I bit down on his earlobe. "I want you now, Dex."

His low groans made me ache for him even more. He pressed his dick against my core, and with one swift movement, he tugged my swimsuit aside and pushed inside me.

Shit.

Fuck.

I wasn't sure who said what, but I didn't care. I just wanted to give him as much pleasure as he'd given me. We made fast, frenzied love. And when we came, we fell over together, clinging to one another like our lives depended on it. In that moment, I realized that I wanted us to always be like this together. So maybe *slow* wasn't what I really wanted after all.

Chapter Eleven

WHAT'S IT GONNA BE!

Charlye

"*I* don't know about this…" I grimaced. "Ooh, that hurts."

Dex kissed the back of my neck while his strong hands massaged my lower back. "Do you trust me?"

I glanced at him over my shoulder. "Of course, I do." I winced. "Dex, go slow."

"Do you want me to stop?"

I buried my face into my hands and grumbled, "No. I need you to keep going."

It could be argued that Justus' wedding was the turning point in my relationship with Dex, but our weekend in Miami had been an awakening of sorts. A reset. We'd made promises to each other to try to work on us.

The last several weeks had been amazing. We'd spent most nights together, making love, talking about everything and nothing. Not that it was a stretch, but I fell harder for him every day, every time he looked at me, every second we were together.

"You ready?" he asked.

I giggled. "No. I'm scared."

He chuckled. Dex had a beautiful, genuine laugh. It did something to me to hear it, to see it, to feel it. It made me want to climb on his lap and do him. But that would be kind of hard to do with these big-ass skates on. And... Most of his family was in close proximity.

Bliss and Blake turned thirty-something. The Youngs made a big deal about birthdays. There were so many of them, but Mama V had made an effort to celebrate each of their "*personal holidays*" as she called them.

As tempting as it was to stay in a bubble with each other, we knew we couldn't hide forever. While everyone we loved was aware of our relationship change, this was our first outing as *more than friends* with Dex's family.

Dex turned me to face him. "You got this."

"If I fall again, I'm leaving." Since we'd arrived at the skating rink an hour ago, I'd already taken two, very public, very embarrassing hard falls. He opened his mouth to speak, probably to give me another pep talk, but I rushed on. "And don't tell me I got this again. I pretty much suck at this."

Bliss zoomed past me, looking all elegant and shit. She waved. "Come on, Char. Get out here and try again."

"She makes me sick," I grumbled, holding on to Dex's arm for dear life. "It's her fault we're here."

For Bliss' birthday, she'd chosen torture. A day full of *fun* activities. Rock climbing, laser tag, and now roller skating. Shooting lasers at each other in the dark wasn't bad, but holding on to tiny little knobs while I climbed a wall was awful. I didn't make it far before I hyperventilated. Dex had to pry my hands away as I held on for dear life.

"Where did Lennox take Blake anyway?" I asked. I couldn't look at him because I was too busy staring at the carpet as we moved slowly. I bit the inside of my cheek, dreading what I knew was coming next. "How did she get out of this?"

Dex tugged me forward, finally pulling me onto the slick floor. "I have no idea." He linked his fingers with mine. "But something tells me she'll come back engaged."

For a moment, I forgot where I was and peered up at him. I paid for that when I nearly toppled over onto my butt. Again. But Dex's arms wrapped around my waist, preventing me from yet another fall. I gripped his shirt. "Thanks."

He kissed my brow. "I got you."

"You better."

"Hold on tight."

When we did one round without so much as a stumble, I finally glanced at him instead of the floor. "I'm doing it." My foot chose that exact moment to betray me, resulting in my knee buckling, which in turn caused a domino effect. I fell first and pulled Dex down with me.

Dex groaned, holding his back. "Damn, Pretty."

Pain shot through my leg. "Ouch! I'm sorry."

Mama V and Papa Stew rolled past us, hand in hand, in sync. They looked like teenagers out there, so smooth, doing little tricks and spins. They didn't even notice that we'd wiped out, but Duke did.

"Shit." Duke stopped in front of us. "Char, I'm only telling you this because you're cute, and you deserve to not look crazy as hell out here. Get off the damn floor and take off those skates."

I glared at Duke. "I hate you."

Duke winked at me. "Sis, you're bad-ass. You can install a switchboard and inspect conduits like a boss. But skating is not your thing."

I cracked up. "I really hate you," I repeated.

Dex stood. "Shut the hell up, bruh." He reached out his hand to me. "Come on, Pretty."

I grabbed his hand and let him help me to my feet, only for me to almost fall yet again. I squeezed his waist. *Oh boy.*

"I told you," Duke teased. "You suck."

"If I didn't have on these skates, I would kick your ass," I remarked, clinging to Dex as he slowly pulled me toward the carpeted area.

Duke followed us. "You tried that in first grade already."

While Dex had always been nice to me, Duke used to be a little shit. Always picking on me, always pointing out when I tripped or had food on my face. It wasn't until he'd entered middle school that our relationship became more sibling-like. Today was no exception. He'd always treated me like a sister. Which was good because he was protective and genuine and kind. Even when he was calling me out or making fun of me. Yep, he got on my damn nerves. But I was sure his sisters felt the same.

Finally, I made it to the round bench near the lockers. My body was on fire, and not in a thoroughly-sexed way. Everything hurt. My arms, my legs, my head, my toes.

"Remind me never to let Bliss talk me into skates again." I sipped on the frozen coke Dex had bought for me.

Dallas, who was munching on a plate of nachos *and* a soft pretzel, giggled. "It won't work. I still can't tell her *no*. And I'm not that nice."

I laughed. "I swear she's like Tinkerbell, sprinkling fairy dust on everyone she encounters."

I'd heard Mama V call Bliss the *Heart* of their family. And I couldn't disagree. The matchmaker by trade had always been so sweet, so open, so giving. She'd excelled in school and in life.

Dex placed one of my legs on his lap and untied my skate. "Bliss has the gift of persuasion."

"Pretty much." Dallas burped. "It's annoying as fuck, though."

"Really, DD?" Dex laughed. "You could at least say excuse me."

"It's not me," Dallas argued. "It's this baby."

"You blame every damn thing on my niece."

"Because it's true. My body is not my own right now. Heartburn, gas, hot flashes, pain in my groin. Pregnancy is not for the faint at heart." She dipped a chip into the cheese sauce. "Hm. This is good." Then, she broke a piece of her pretzel off and popped it into her mouth.

"Damn, sis." Asa slid into the booth next to his sister and swiped one of her nachos. "You're eating again? Didn't you just eat a slice of pizza and a hot dog?"

"Hey." Dallas smacked his hand. "Don't touch my food, shit."

Asa shook his head. "Yo' ass is greedy as hell."

An argument ensued between Dallas and Asa about food, personal training, and... *Similac versus breast feeding*? And Dex had seemingly tuned them out.

I leaned closer. "What just happened here?"

Dex motioned for my other leg and removed that skate as well. "Dallas thinks she's the boss."

A chip hit Dex in the nose. "I heard that," Dallas said. "And I *am* the boss."

Grinning, Dex, threw the same chip back at her and it

landed in her hair. I covered my smile, but Asa fell on the floor laughing.

Dallas caught my attempt to hide my amusement and said, "Chicks over dicks, Char. You already know this."

I choked on my drink. Patting my chest, I told her to warn me next time. "You're so silly for that."

Dex kissed me, then stood. "I'll turn the skates in, and we can go."

Once he was out of earshot, I met the amused eyes of Dallas and Asa. "What?" I asked.

Dallas smirked. "Asa, leave."

Asa snickered. "I'm not going anywhere, sis."

Unphased, Dallas said. "You absolutely are getting the hell out of here. Or I'll tell all your dirty little secrets."

The two siblings stared at each other for a moment. Asa broke first, "What do you know?" he asked.

"It doesn't matter, does it? Especially if you leave."

Asa muttered a curse. "You get on my damn nerves."

The gleam in Dallas' eye returned. "I love you, brother." She kissed his cheek. "See you in a minute?"

Without another word, Asa walked away, grumbling something I couldn't quite make out.

Curious, I leaned forward. "What is his secret?" I whispered.

Dallas waved me off. "Girl, I don't know. But Asa's so damn secretive, I knew I could get him to leave if I said that."

"Well played."

"Enough about my little brother. Spill."

I'd managed to avoid this conversation up until now. Every time we'd seen anyone in his family, Dex had been with me. But I'd seen the looks, the promise in his sisters' eyes. This day had been coming for a long time. They were super protective of each other, had always been ready to dog walk anyone who messed with one of their own. The stories of epic cuss outs and fights in the name of defending a sibling were well known in our town. I'd even witnessed several incidents in my teenage years, mostly because Blake liked a good beatdown. I'd even heard about a bar fight just last year. I wasn't nervous though, or even intimidated. Justus and Elise were the same way.

"What do you want to know?" I asked.

She arched a brow. "Are you sure?"

I tapped the table. "If you're asking if I want to be with your brother, I do."

"I'm asking if you're sure."

I answered the question with one of my own. "Do you think I'd be here if I wasn't?"

Dallas was Dex's sister, but I considered her a good friend. We'd graduated in the same high school class, attended Hampton together freshman year. She'd helped me fix my life on more than one occasion over the years and had kept my confidence. In fact, Dallas was the only person who knew about Jack. She never judged me. She simply hopped on a flight and flew her ass down to Atlanta to make sure I was okay.

"I love you, Char," she said. "You're family. If you weren't sure, I wouldn't love you any less. But I will tell you what Dex deserves. My brother does a good job ensuring that all of us are taken care of. He's clutch for real. I just need him to have someone that is willing to walk through fire for him too. That's all."

I met her gaze. "It's still new."

"You're in the honeymoon phase of a new relationship, new expectations for each other. But these are not *new* feelings."

In Miami, I'd told Dex I was sure. And I was. *I am*. I trusted him. I adored him. *I love him*. Still, there were real considerations that we hadn't talked about. I hadn't decided to move to Michigan. My entire family was in transition. Everything had changed after Julia died. Harper accepted a job in Minnesota. Justus and Isis were planning a family. I suspected Elise was pregnant but holding off on the announcement. My mother had mentioned downsizing her house or moving to Atlanta to be closer to us. And I couldn't stay there indefinitely without a plan. I hadn't quit my job. Hell, I hadn't even talked to my boss about any of this. I'd been so distracted, so engrossed in Dex that I'd failed to be logical. If this was going to work, we needed to have that conversation.

Dallas reached over and placed her hand on mine. She gave me a gentle squeeze. "Maybe you two need to have a talk? Just sayin'."

I nodded. She was right. "Definitely." My phone buzzed. I glanced at the screen, cringing at the number. My boss had been trying to reach me for several days.

Dallas stood. "I'll let you handle that."

I answered the phone. "Hi. I'm so sorry, Carl. It's been crazy."

Carl Matthews had taken me under his wing from the moment I entered his business and announced that I wanted to learn from him. He didn't have kids, so he'd passed down all his knowledge to me. Recently, he'd encouraged me to step outside of my comfort zone and take a more active role in his business. He'd even suggested that I set up the non-profit to help other black women break into the field.

"I'm glad you picked up," Carl said. "How are you? How is your mom?"

"She's hanging in there."

"Good. I know you're on leave and I wouldn't call if it wasn't important."

My stomach dropped and I sat up straight. "Is everything okay?"

"We're fine, Char," he assured me. "I've just made some decisions that I'd like to speak to you about. Can you come to Atlanta in the next few weeks so we can talk in person?"

"Sure?" I moistened my lips. "Can you give me a hint?"

"Absolutely. Angel and I have talked. I'm going to retire at the end of the year. And I'd like you to take over the business."

I blinked. "What?"

"Char, you're basically a much younger me with hair. I don't trust anyone else with CM Electric."

"I'm… Wow." Off in the distance, I spotted Dex standing with Asa and Duke. They were laughing and it was a beautiful sight. *He* was beautiful. "Um… I don't know what to say, Carl." *I don't know what to do.*

"I hope you'll at least consider it, Charlye."

"Of course, I will." I swallowed past a lump that had formed in my throat. "I'll make arrangements to fly back in the next few weeks."

"Thanks. Talk to you soon."

I ended the call just as Dex approached me. "Ready, Pretty?"

The long hours and sore fingers, the uncertainty I'd faced when I decided to become an electrician, the doubts from many of my male colleagues had been worth it to hear Carl say he trusted me with his business. And he'd given me so much of his time, so much guidance, that I couldn't imagine telling him *no*. Which was a problem because… I peered up at Dex.

He frowned. "Are you okay?"

No. Because if I accepted Carl's offer, where would that

leave us. I glanced up and met Dallas' knowing gaze. Then, I looked at Dex and forced a smile. "I'm ready."

He reached out and I slipped my hand in his, letting him help me up. "Hungry?"

I shook my head, brushed my hand over the back of my neck. "Sure," I lied. Food was the last thing on my mind. "Actually, I'm kind of tired. Back to your place?"

Dex tilted his head, studied me for a long moment. But he didn't question me. He simply said, "Okay."

We said our goodbyes with hugs and promises to get together soon. And as we headed back to his house, I couldn't shake the feeling that this latest development could make or break us.

Dexter

"ARE you going to let me in?"

Charlye jumped into my arms. "You're here." She wrapped her legs around my waist and peppered my face with kisses as I carried her inside her condo.

She'd been in Atlanta for the last week. It had only been seven days, but it felt like thirty. Since Miami, we'd spent most nights together. Being without her for even a day felt like an eternity. I backed her into the wall. "Miss me?"

She tugged my shirt off and brushed her lips over mine. "So much. Orgasm me."

A smirk tugged at my lips. "As you wish."

I swiveled and we fell back onto the couch, with her straddling my lap. I lifted her nightgown up and off as she unbuckled my belt. Sitting up, I brushed my thumb over one of her nipples before taking the other one in my mouth, sucking until she begged me never to stop. Flipping her over, I rested on top of her, feathered my finger over her cheek. "So beautiful."

She beamed up at me. "You always say that."

"Because it's true."

Charlye kissed me, pushing my jeans down and wrapped her fist around my dick. I rested my forehead on hers and thrust inside. "Because you're mine," I whispered as I made slow love to her. "*This* is mine."

"Yes," she moaned. "All yours."

I could spend the rest of my life making love to her. *Loving* her. Years of wanting her, of dreaming of her, had been nothing compared to *being* with her in this way. I was lost in her, consumed by her. And it felt better than anything else I'd ever felt.

She cried out her release first, with my name on her lips. Then, I let go.

Moments later, we were seated on the couch, legs entwined as we shared a plate of leftover spaghetti. Charlye had successfully made the transition from burnt noodles to spaghetti artist in the years we were apart. And it was even better the next day.

"If I'd known you were coming, I would've cooked something else."

I twisted my fork, wrapping a mound of noodles around it. "This is perfect."

"How's the book coming?"

The other day, we'd video chatted while I worked on my next book. The deadline for my full outline was fast approaching, but I had no doubt I would meet it. Just needed to tweak a few things. Spring was in the air and my family was gearing up for softball season. The last thing I wanted to do was be stuck in the house writing during opening day. "It's going. I should be done next week, before our first game."

"Oh good. I'll be on the bleachers cheering you on."

I chuckled. I'd tried to get Char to play a few games with us, only to be slapped with a hard *no*. "Sure you don't want to join us?"

"Yeah, no. Y'all are not gon' have me out there looking foolish."

I tapped her nose. "You would never look foolish to me." Her expression softened. I couldn't quite put my finger on it, but I sensed she was sad. *Regret?* It wasn't the first time she'd looked at me that way. Something had shifted between us at Bliss' birthday celebration a few weeks ago. She opened her mouth like she wanted to talk to me, but instead of speaking, she averted her gaze. "Char?"

She looked at me then, tears swimming in her brown eyes. "I have something to tell you."

My stomach roiled. I set my fork down. "What is it?"

Her eyes flitted back and forth between mine. "Carl offered me an amazing opportunity, but it would mean I couldn't move to Michigan."

Suddenly, everything made sense. It was regret I'd read in her eyes. We hadn't brought up her living situation since Naija's birthday party. I'd been so distracted by her, so caught up in her, that I'd done the exact opposite of what I should've done. I ignored the warning signs because I wanted her. I couldn't see past my desire for her. It all boiled down to one thing. No matter how right it felt, our timing was wrong. Because she'd made her decision. She planned to stay in Atlanta.

"Dex, I haven't given him an answer yet," she insisted.

"But you've already decided?"

"He wants to sell me his business."

Even though I knew what was coming next, even as my own emotions threatened to choke me with their intensity, I couldn't help but be proud of her. She'd worked her ass off and now she was finally getting what she deserved. "That's amazing."

"It is." She flashed a sad smile. "Dex, I—"

"A few months ago, you asked me what I wanted," I interrupted.

"And you told me you wanted me." Her chin trembled. "Does this change that?"

"Never," I admitted. "But more than anything, I've always only wanted you to be happy." A tear spilled from her eyes, and she brushed it off. "What kind of man would I be if I didn't tell you to jump on this opportunity?"

"You wouldn't."

"Exactly."

"But I haven't decided yet, Dex," she argued. "Mom decided to stay in Michigan for a while, and I don't want to abandon her. And I certainly don't want to lose you. I can work anywhere. I can partner with Preston or focus on my non-profit. I think I could be happy there."

"You *think*?"

She frowned. "Yeah, I…" Her shoulders fell. "I think so."

The need to put some distance between us made me stand and pace the floor. I took a moment, counted to ten several times. I wasn't angry with her, but I had to fight the strong urge to beg her to stay with me. Because I wouldn't force her to choose. "Here's what I know," I said finally. "I *know* I love you."

Her eyes widened. "You do?"

"I'm so in love with you, Char. I probably always have been. Time and distance didn't change that simple fact. It seems it just lay dormant until I saw you at Justus' wedding, until I kissed you. I *know* my life is better with you. But I also *know* that you just lost Julia, and you broke up with your boyfriend. I *know* I'm not moving to Atlanta. And I knew better. I knew better than to start a relationship with—"

"Don't," she warned. She stood, tossing her napkin onto the table. "Don't do this, Dex. You're making it seem like I don't have a mind of my own, like I'm just out here being reckless with your feelings. And mine. I'm not the same person that I was in high school or even college. My life hasn't been a bed of roses. I've done some things I'm not proud of, but I'm very capable of deciding on my own. I've been doing it for over a decade without you. I don't need you to shrink me. I need you to trust me." She sighed. "But you don't, do you?"

I lifted my eyes, held her gaze. "Char, you—"

"You don't trust me not to run from you."

"That's not true," I told her.

"Then, what's the problem? I'm standing here telling you that I want this to work and you're pushing me away."

"That's not what I'm doing, Char. Three years down the line, when you're in Michigan and you realize that you should've stayed here, that your life is in Atlanta… I don't want you to resent me."

"What happened to taking every day as it comes? Why are you skipping ahead to some point in time that we don't even know will exist?"

"Because…" I let out a deep breath. "You *think* you can be happy in Michigan, but I need you to *know*." I slipped on my pants and my shirt.

"Where are you going?" she asked.

"Maybe we need to take some time. You can think about what you want, and I can…"

"Dex?" She walked toward me. "Don't leave. We can talk about this."

"*I* need some time, Char." I cupped her face in my hands and kissed her. "I'll call you."

Then, as much as I wanted to stay, as much as I wanted to lose myself in her body, in her scent, in her voice, I left.

Chapter Twelve

CAN YOU STAND THE RAIN?

Charlye

*I*t had been hours since Dex left, and I still couldn't believe the sharp turn his surprise visit had taken. I knew we'd have to talk about the job, that I'd have to decide where I wanted to be. But I never expected the conversation to end like it did.

"Here?" Elise handed me a glass of wine. "You need this."

I gulped the Merlot down. "Thanks."

"Have you heard from him?"

I shook my head. "Justus said he's with Duke."

Elise sat in my recliner and tucked her feet under her butt. "Are you ready to talk?"

"I'm not sure I know what to say," I admitted. "It feels... I don't know."

A soft knock on the door drew my attention away from my sister. *Maybe it's Dex?* I set my glass down and hurried to the door, pulling it open. My shoulders fell when I realized it was Justus.

"Damn, baby sis. You're not happy to see me?" He pulled me into a hug. "I just wanted to check on you." He rubbed the top of my head and placed a kiss to my temple. "You alright?"

I closed my sweater to ward off the chill that had set in since Dex walked out. "I don't know." I shuffled back to my spot on the couch. "Have you talked to him?"

Justus nodded. "For a minute. His father is in town. They're all together."

"I didn't know Papa Stew was here." Dex and I hadn't had a chance to really catch up when he'd arrived earlier.

"Do you still have some of that spaghetti?" Justus pulled my refrigerator open and peered inside. "Ooh." He held up the dill vegetable dip I'd made earlier. "I need some of this."

"Go ahead."

While Justus scooped a lot of dip onto his plate, Elise asked, "Okay, so let's talk about it. What happened, sis?"

Justus paused, met my gaze.

I shrugged. "I told you... I told him about Carl and the business. He said he was proud of me. Right before he told me he loved me. After that, everything went downhill."

Elise smiled. "He told you that?"

"He did." I gave my brother and sister an abridged version of the events leading up to the we-need-time speech. "And he left." When my siblings didn't speak, I finally glanced at both, only to find them looking at every-thing *but* me. "What?"

Justus bit into a carrot. "You tell her, Elise."

Elise let out a heavy sigh. "So... You told him that you *think* you would be happy in Michigan?"

I stared directly at my sister. "Yes, I think I can be happy in Michigan."

"You *think*?" Justus challenged. "Or you *know*?"

"Babe, Dex is grown-grown," Elise said. "He knows what he wants. And he's at the point in his life where he needs the woman he loves to know too." She held up her hand when I opened my mouth to speak. "This is not to say that he wasn't being a little asshole-y about the whole thing, but put yourself in his shoes. He loves you. Did you tell him you loved him too?"

My stomach fell. "No."

"*Do* you love him?" Elise asked.

"I do," I whispered. "You know I do."

"Maybe you should tell him that," Justus joined us in the living room and sat down on the couch next to me. "Maybe he needs to hear it."

There was no doubt in my mind that I'd messed this up by not telling Dex how much he meant to me, that I loved him with everything in me. "Okay, so I fucked up."

"It's not too late to fix it," Elise said. "But I have a question for you?"

"Okay."

"Do you want to decline Carl's offer and move to Michigan?"

"I think…" I trailed off as realization dawned on me. I wanted to take over Carl's business. When we'd met earlier in the week, I found his proposal to be fair and exciting. While I enjoyed my time in Michigan, I couldn't deny that I missed working. I loved my job. "Why can't I have both Dex *and* the business?"

"Is that realistic?" Justus asked.

"Carl is giving me his business. Who's to say I can't expand to the Ann Arbor area. I don't have to be in

Atlanta. I can hire someone else, train another black woman to take over here."

Justus smirked. "No one can say that but you."

"You'd help me on the business end of things?"

"Anything you need," he promised.

"You do know it's cold as hell in Michigan," Elise quipped. "Be very sure."

"It is, but I never feel cold when I'm with Dex." Once again, Julia's words came to mind. Finally, I shared what she'd told me with Justus and Elise.

"Wow." Elise dabbed at her eyes. "I miss her."

Justus cleared his throat. "She was the shit. She is missed."

"That's why I *know* I'll be happy there," I said. "Because I'll be with him."

"Damn, Char," Elise cried. "I'm going to miss you."

Justus grumbled a curse. "What the hell is wrong with you? You can hop your ass on the first flight out whenever you want to see her."

I glared at my brother. "Really, Justus? Stop being an asshole."

"Where is Harper's weird ass when I need him to be another man in the room?" he said. "Stop crying."

"I'm just pregnant," my sister announced.

I gasped. "Elise! I knew it."

Her chin trembled. "I was waiting to tell you both at dinner on Sunday."

"Are you happy?" I asked.

"Very," she replied. "We plan on telling Ellis tonight. He's going to be an awesome big brother."

I shot Justus a look. "You next?"

He waggled his eyebrows. "We're certainly putting in the work."

I scowled. "Ew."

He wrapped his arm around my neck and shook me playfully. "Hey, you're sleeping with my best friend. You can hear about my sex life."

I cracked up. "That's nasty. *No.*"

"Now I have to go shopping for baby stuff with Jay," Elise complained. "Lord, help me. He's going to police everything I buy. I'll have to ship my Amazon boxes to your house, Justus."

"I'm going to be there every step of the way, even from Michigan," I assured her. "You can ship your stuff to me, and we'll just pretend you got everything at the baby shower I'm going to throw you."

"See." Justus shook his head in mock disgust. "Y'all be scheming."

"Just pretend you didn't hear that, lil' brother," Elise chirped. "So it's decided, Char?"

"Yeah," I confirmed. "Dex and I still need to talk, but I'm ready to take that step with him."

Elise slid off the chair and shuffled over to us on her knees. "That's what I wanted to hear."

I wiped the tears from her face. "Please stop. You're going to make me cry, and I don't want to have bags under my eyes when I see Dex." I hugged her.

Justus wrapped his arms around both of us. "Y'all some punks for real. Get ya' shit together and wash your ass. Duke just texted me his location."

Dexter

"Bruh, you're wrong as hell."

156

I paused, cue stick in hand. Standing to my full height, I glared at my brother. "I don't remember asking for your opinion."

"When has that ever stopped me from giving it?" He finished off his beer. For the last few hours, we'd been at a bar near my brother's house, shooting pool and talking shit. Dad had just left, and now it was just me and Duke.

I didn't bother arguing with him because he was right. I hadn't been gone for two minutes before I'd realized I was a fuckin' asshole. I wouldn't give my brother the satisfaction, though. "Why am I wrong?"

"Did you at least tell her you loved her?"

I lined up my shot again. "Who said anything about love?" Then, I took it, sending my ball into the corner pocket.

"Shit, man. I shared a damn amniotic sac with your ass for nine months. I can feel that shit whenever Charlye's around."

I barked out a laugh. "You're dumb as hell."

"It's true, though."

I also didn't bother denying my feelings. "It is. And I did tell her."

He clasped my shoulder. "'Bout time."

"Does it really matter how I feel, though, if Charlye isn't ready?" I asked. "I've never pushed her before. I'm not going to start today."

"Did you ask her to stay?"

"Why would I do that?"

Duke lifted his hands. "Because you want to be with her? What the hell?"

"It's a good opportunity for her."

"It's an amazing opportunity for her," he agreed.

"Again, why would I ask her to stay?"

"Why wouldn't you come to her?" he challenged.

"Seriously, bruh. If the woman you love wants to be in Atlanta, why wouldn't you move heaven and earth to be here with her?"

The truth of the matter was plain to see, and despite my attempts to hide it, even from myself, my brother had recognized it. I rubbed a hand over my face. "Fuck."

"Instead of sitting here with me, yo' ass needs to be planning your move. Bruh, you're a damn relationship coach. You can do that shit anywhere. Hell, you can move to Alaska and help women get fucked."

I snickered. "You never stop talking, do you?

"Not when I see you fucking up."

"Maybe you should pay more attention to your own shit."

"Trust me, I could never run away from my own shit. But this isn't about me. I'm talking about you. You've loved this girl since she had braces and messy-ass braids. And you've spent the last few hours maintaining this stance that Charlye isn't ready. That *she's* scared, that *she'll* run."

I hadn't realized that I'd said that much to my brother since I'd barged in on him trying to get rid of his date that afternoon. "Because it's true."

"Bull shit. You should know that every woman is not the same. What works for one doesn't necessarily work for others. Some women need time to process a breakup or a death. But some women know what the hell they want. You act like you and Charlye don't know each other."

"Maybe we don't." My response sounded weak to my own ears, so I knew my brother would see right through it.

"Bull shit," he repeated. "Years have passed. You've both experienced things that have shaped who you are today. But you're still the same people you were that summer after we graduated. You loved her, and she loved you. The only difference was she was scared then. She's not scared now, Dex. She's been making all the moves. She asked *you* to help her. She asked *you* if you wanted to explore more. She asked *you* to take things slow with her. She told *you* that she could make her own decisions."

I set my beer down on the table. It was my fifth or sixth since we'd been there, not including the two shots of bourbon I'd downed before we even left Duke's house. The fact that my brother knew all those details confirmed that I talked too damn much—while under the influence. It was time to slow that down.

As if he knew what I was thinking, Duke smirked. "Too late, brotha. You spilled all yo' shit."

I asked the waitress to bring a pitcher of water. "I'm done. With the beer and this conversation."

He waved me off. "I'm not listening to that shit, because I'm not done. All along you've been accusing Charlye of being what *you* are."

"Shut the fuck up," I growled.

"You're scared as hell."

I stepped to Duke, ready to choke the shit out of him. Only my anger wasn't at my brother, but at myself. Still, I needed to take it out on someone, and his chin looked strong enough to absorb my fist. He didn't back down, though. He never did.

Dad rushed back in, feeling on his shirt and his pockets. "I think I left my wallet." His eyes darted back and forth between us. "What the hell…?" He approached us, clasped each of our shoulders. "Neutral corners." The command was clear, and we did as he said. Turning to me, Dad said, "I don't know what's going on, but I can't imagine any reason you would be ready to fight your brother in public. Dex, get your shit together." Then, he faced Duke. "Sometimes you need to shut the hell up." He let out a heavy sigh. "What happened?"

Duke smiled. "I'm good, Pops. Dex is the angry one. But he's probably more pissed at himself than me."

I sat down on a nearby stool and took a deep breath. "He's right, Dad. He didn't do anything but tell me the truth." And because the truth hurt, I was ready to take it out on him. "I'm the one who fucked up."

"And?" Dad questioned. "Fix it. Is this about Charlye?"

I nodded. "I overreacted. Because I'm…" *Scared as hell to lose her.* "I fucked up."

"Good thing she's standing over there." He pointed behind me. "Tell her that."

I turned around, and sure enough, Charlye was standing there, a tentative smile on her full lips. "Char?"

She let out a nervous giggle and waved. "Hi." She approached me. "Can we talk?"

Chapter Thirteen

PRAY YOU CATCH ME

Charlye

"Charlye!" Papa Stew embraced me. "It's good to see you."

"You too." I swallowed, glancing at Dex again. "I hope I'm not interrupting anything important."

Papa Stew shook his head. "Not at all. Duke and I were just leaving."

"Right." Duke approached me and gave me a kiss on my cheek. "What's up?"

"Nothing much." I shrugged. "Ready for Spring."

"You'll have to come to opening day," Papa Stew suggested. "We have a lot of fun. I'm trying to get Duke to commit to more games this year."

Duke snickered. "That would be a negative, Pops. I'll do my normal two games, thanks." He looked at Dex. "We good?"

Dex nodded and the brothers gave each other their signature dap. "Yeah."

Clasping Dex's shoulder, Duke said, "Love you, man."

"Love you too."

I said my goodbyes to Duke and Papa Stew, then turned to Dex. Frowning, I asked, "What happened? Are you okay?"

He sighed. "Let's just say Duke almost got his ass packed up."

"Why?"

"He talks too much." He lifted his eyes. "Enough about him, though."

I nodded for no other reason than to stall. On the way there, I'd rehearsed an entire speech, one right out of a smutty romance novel. But I couldn't remember a single thing I'd come up with in that moment.

"I'm glad you came," Dex said, letting me off the hook. "I don't want to talk here, though. Can we go back to your place?"

I squeezed the belt of my purse. "Sure."

The ride home was quiet, no small talk, no anything. Silent and awkward. I'd even forgotten to turn on the music. Walking into my house felt like I was walking a plank. Despite my bravado earlier with Justus and Elise, my confidence slipped as soon as they'd left. Although I liked to think I'd made a lot of progress in that area, apparently, I still had work to do.

On the way to the bar, visions of every negative scenario plagued me. I found myself questioning my ability to make this relationship work.

How is this going to work?

I knew Dex hated long distance relationships. He liked proximity and I didn't blame him. Because I did too. Even if I did expand the business, that could take years of commuting back and forth, weekend visits, missed flights or lacking video chats. Add to that, my track record wasn't the best when it came to longevity with men. *I could fuck this up.*

What if he doesn't believe me?

It was clear he didn't trust me not to leave. That was my fault because I'd run from him before. Back then, it had never occurred to me that *I* could break someone's heart, that *I* could be someone's unrequited crush. Just thinking about it made me ache for him because I knew that pain all too well. Dex was one of the strongest people I knew, but everyone struggled with something.

Dex was the whole shit. Everything I've ever wanted in a partner—giving and kind. Gentle. A perfect gentleman and a fierce protector. He was low-key a genius. I respected him. I wanted him. *I love him.*

I locked the door and took a few cleansing breaths. That shit didn't work, though. And I felt nervous, hesitant to say something that would derail my best intentions.

Again, Dex spoke first. "I was wrong. I thought I knew what was best for you, and I failed to consider what *you* want, how *you* feel. This whole time, I've been trying to convince you that you're worth more than you realize. I wanted you to know what it felt like to be chased, to be put above all else. I did it for many reasons, but mostly because you deserve it. Then, the moment things got hard, I used that as an excuse to walk away. I told myself that it was better for me to leave than to get left. I let my inner asshole take over because I was scared."

The lump in my throat made it difficult to swallow. I held back tears that I'd promised myself I wouldn't let fall. At least, not before I'd communicated everything he needed to know. "Scared of me? Of us?"

"Scared of losing you." My eyes flashed to his. His

expression softened. "Duke pointed it out today. As a result, I wanted to kick his ass. I didn't want to see it, but he was right. Sometime between Justus' wedding and today, probably even before that, I realized that I would be wrecked if I couldn't spend the rest of my life loving you. 'Cause I didn't have to *fall* in love with you. I've *been* in love with you. And I put my own shit, my own fears on you. That wasn't fair." He inched closer and trailed his fingers over my cheek. "Char, you've always told me you felt unworthy, unwanted. But that's the last thing you are. You're everything, and because of that, you're worthy of me crossing state lines to be with you."

Damn. I let out a slow, measured breath. The words I'd rehearsed earlier came back to me in a rush. I knew what I had to do; I knew what I had to say.

"To think I was going to tell you the same thing," I confessed with a soft laugh.

He smirked. "You were going to cross state lines for me?"

"I had a plan and everything."

Dex chuckled. "Tell me all about it."

I shook my head. "Not right now. I have something I need to say to you." I cleared my throat. "No one has ever made me feel like you do. I don't think you realize how much you mean to me." I pressed my lips to his. "You check all of my boxes. Allow me to appreciate you."

He laughed then, and it felt like he'd bathed me in warmth, filled me with his heat.

I nipped his chin. "Because you inspire me." I picked up his hand and kissed his palm. "Because you've never tried to change me." I ran my finger over the dimple on his right cheek. "Because you're smart." I smoothed my hands over his chest. "Because you're my best friend." I tugged his shirt off. "Because you're fine as hell." Chuckling, he rested his forehead against mine. I slid his belt off. "Because you're strong and I feel safe with you. And you can pick me up with no effort."

He grinned. "You're silly for that."

"Because you were my first." I pushed his pants down. "Because you make me laugh." I brushed my lips over his heart. "Because you make me feel warm even on the coldest days." I wrapped my arms around his waist. "Because you're everything." I searched his eyes. "Because I love you."

His lips captured mine. I poured everything I had into that kiss. All of my heart, all of my soul.

"I don't know where we'll end up," I continued. "What I *do* know is that I want to be with you. I *do* know that I love you. So much."

Dex cradled my face in his hands and planted the sweetest kiss to my lips. He arched a brow. "Does this mean we're not going to go slow anymore?"

I cracked up. "I don't think we ever went slow." I smirked. "Now..." I hopped into his arms. "Orgasm me, please."

He carried me to my bedroom, lowered me onto the bed, and pressed his dick to my core. "As you wish."

We made slow, lazy love. When we climaxed, we did so together. Always together. And I knew that was where I wanted to be. Forever.

———

Dexter

Summer, this year

. . .

THE TEXT MESSAGES had been coming nonstop all morning. In two short hours, my siblings managed to discuss everything from baby spit up and Blake's upcoming wedding to the Young Family retreat and potato salad. Now, they were talking about the baker we hired for Mom and Dad's anniversary party that evening.

Blake: *I don't have time for her fuckin' feelings. We hired her to do a damn job. Tonight.*

Bliss: *Just call her back and apologize.*

Apparently, the woman hadn't answered any of Blake's calls because my sister had insulted her at the cake-tasting they'd had the other day. Bliss had spent hours trying to smooth things over, but the lady wanted an apology from Blake.

Blake: *I said I was sorry yesterday.*

Dallas: *No, you told her you were sorry her cake sucked.*

They went round and round for the next several minutes, but Blake was adamant. Asa chimed in next: *The party is tonight. Duke, can you handle it?*

It took a few minutes, but Duke finally responded: *Hell no. I told y'all not to hire her anyway. B is right. That cake was trash. It was hard and tasted like old cornbread.*

Charlye came out the bathroom. It had taken a while, but she'd finally stopped emerging from the bathroom fully clothed in the mornings. The simple fact that she was only wearing a towel was a huge step. "Are y'all still at it?" She stared at the closet door where she'd hung two different outfits. "It's been hours." I gave her a quick rundown of the conversation. "Yikes. Cornbread?" She grabbed the black dress, brought it closer to the bed, and held it up. "This one?"

I shook my head. "Wear the one you pulled out last night."

"It's white?"

"So? It's August. And it's your birthday."

"You know I don't care about that. We're here for your parents."

Charlye was hardheaded. Birthdays were huge in my family, but it was like pulling teeth just to get her to let me take her to dinner. "But it's your day too."

"I know." She nibbled on her lower lip. "Do I really have to wear a dress, though? It's not formal. I can wear the slacks."

I yanked the towel off and pulled her closer to me. "It's your birthday. Wear the dress."

She wrapped her arms around my neck and kissed me. "It might be too tight."

"It's not."

I brushed my finger over her clit, enjoying her sharp intake of air. "Dex, we have to get dressed." She groaned when I took a taut nipple in my mouth and tugged it with my teeth. "We're going to be late."

Maya had planned a brunch since we were all in town. The matriarch of the family was slowly getting back to her life and finally made the decision to stop practicing law. While she'd continue teaching at the Law School, she wanted the flexibility to travel, to enjoy her life.

"We will." I pulled her on top of me and rolled over. "Later," I murmured against her ear. "Much later."

Two orgasms later, she moaned. "I'm going to be no good today." She kissed me and slid off the bed. "I have to hop in the shower again."

Once she disappeared into the bathroom, I glanced at my phone. I had at least fifty new messages, all about the cake lady. I scrolled up to catch up on the latest messages and snickered at the last one.

Blake: *Dex!!! Chime in, muthafucka.*

Even though she'd sent it an hour ago, I finally responded: *Go to Costco. Save some money.*

Dallas: *That ship has long sailed. Cake situation, handled. Are you back?*

Our flight had landed late last night, and we'd driven straight to my house. After careful consideration and many pros and cons lists, Charlye and I had settled on Atlanta—*and* Michigan. Her idea to expand the business had sparked renewed interest in Carl, and he'd postponed his retirement for a few years. The plan was to launch in Ann Arbor and prepare one of the current employees to take a more active role at the Atlanta site.

Charlye would split her time in Michigan and Georgia to allow Carl more family time with his wife and his great-nieces. It would also give me more time to determine the next step for my business.

I texted that I was in town, then added: *Stop texting.*

For some reason, Dallas requested to change the call to FaceTime. Seconds later, my siblings were on the screen. I kept the camera off.

"Blake?" Dallas called. "What is wrong with you?"

The murderous look in Blake's eyes told me she was ready to fight. Her hair was piled high on her head, and she had something green on her face. "Really, Dallas? You're the worst kind of worker. Always wanting a face-to-face when you could've sent an email. I have shit to do today."

"I hope that involves cleaning that shit off your face, sis," Dallas retorted, unphased by Blake's ire. She was holding my niece, Dominique, in her arms. We'd only been gone for a month, and it seemed like she'd already changed so much. "I miss seeing your faces."

"Aw." Bliss beamed. "Motherhood has softened you. I'm proud."

Dallas raised a brow. "Not really. I'll still cut a bitch."

"With what?" Paityn asked. "A bottle?"

Everyone laughed at Dallas' expense. She held up a middle finger. "Anyway, I called to let you know that the parents have requested that we be on time for every event on the agenda today. There's a lot going on."

"Again," Blake said. "A text. This could've been a text. Y'all all get on my nerves. Dex, what the hell are you doing?"

"Right?" Bliss said. "We need to see your face too."

Asa was running on the treadmill. "You never get on my nerves, Blake."

Blake pressed her lips together. "You get on my nerves every day. If you weren't my brother, we wouldn't be here. Because I would've kicked your ass a long time ago."

Charlye came out of the bathroom again. This time she was naked. And… my dick appreciated that. Now hard and horny again, I beckoned to her with my finger.

She winked. "Nope."

"Dex, show yourself," Blake shouted. "You're the only one I want to see."

"You'll see me tonight," I told her.

Looking fresh and bubbly like always, Bliss pointed out, "Duke's not on camera either."

"Because I don't want to see y'all asses this early," Duke murmured. "And I'm working."

Paityn yawned. "Dallas, Blake is right. This FaceTime wasn't even necessary."

Blake leaned in like she could see something different. "Are you with someone?"

Frowning, Paityn said, "Me? Bishop is right here."

"Not you, Sissy. Duke's ass," Blake clarified.

"No," Bliss answered for him. "He better not have someone in my house."

Duke groaned. "I should've stayed my black ass at Dex's house. The last time I checked my mother's name was Victoria. And I'm not even at *your* house anymore."

Bliss rolled her eyes. "You left? After you rolled up in here at four in the morning waking Naija up? Where did you go?"

"Mama?" Naija appeared on the screen next. "Hi." She waved at all of us, her plump cheeks full of something. She held up a blueberry and stuffed it into her already full mouth.

"Fuck," Duke grumbled. "Damn-it. I have to go."

"Fuck," Naija repeated.

Everybody cracked up except for Bliss, who covered her daughter's mouth and glared at the camera. "Duke, you're the reason Naija is walking around here shouting curse words and laughing. You're staying at Mom's tonight. I'm done."

"Unca Dukie," Naija said.

Blake giggled. "That's right, Unca Dukie. Get yo' shit and bounce. Corrupting my pretty niece."

"Shit," Naija shouted.

Bliss turned red. "I'm hanging up. Apparently, y'all can't have a curse-free conversation in front of little ears."

Duke finally turned his camera on. "She's going to learn anyway, damn-it."

Naija clapped. "Unca Dukie."

"Uncle Duke, baby doll," my brother corrected. "Uncle. Duke."

"Dukie," Naija repeated. "Dukie."

Blake laughed, falling off the screen. "That's right,

baby doll. Way to recognize when a man is full of shit. I'm gonna teach you a thing or two."

Charlye giggled. "Y'all are crazy."

Bliss perked up. "Is that Char? Happy Birthday!" She started our family's signature birthday song, and everyone joined in.

Once they were done singing, my now fully clothed girlfriend leaned over and smiled at the camera. "Hey, fam. Thank you."

"Did Justus make it in?" Asa asked.

The whole Burke-Winters family had come to town for the anniversary party. Even Charles had received an invitation, which was a huge feat since my mother couldn't stand him. But since Julia died, Char's dad had put in the effort to mend his relationship with his ex-wife and children, and my mother recognized that.

"Yeah," Char answered. "They should be at Mom's."

"Time to end this boring-ass unnecessary conversation," Duke said. "I have to finish something." He dropped off without another word.

After that, like dominoes we all fell off the call. I managed to convince Charlye to join me in the shower, which delayed our departure by another hour and a half. But soon we were on our way to Maya's house. When we arrived, there was a line of cars in front of the house.

Charlye glanced at me, then back at the house. She seemed slightly confused. "Why are there so many cars here? I thought it was just us."

I hunched a shoulder. "I don't know." The lie was a necessary one, so it wasn't hard to say. I knew what was happening inside because I'd planned it.

We walked up to the door. She smiled at me. "You look good, babe."

I pressed a kiss to her lips. "You do too. Glad you wore the white dress, Pretty."

She tugged at the belt. "I'm still not sure about it."

I let my gaze travel from her eyes to her painted toes. "I am."

Maya opened the door. "You're here. And you're late."

Charlye pointed at me. "His fault."

"Hi, Dex." Maya embraced me. "Missed you. Come in."

Charlye walked in first, not noticing the knowing glance Maya gave me as I followed her inside. "Mom, why are there so many cars outside?" Charlye dropped her purse on a table near the door.

"What cars?" Maya asked.

As we headed toward the kitchen, Charlye said, "There's a line of cars in front of the house. Did you invite—?"

"Surprise!"

Charlye yelped, jumping back into me. I wrapped my arms around her waist and squeezed. "Happy Birthday, Pretty," I whispered against her ear.

She whirled around. "Dex!" She smacked my shoulder. "You tricked me!"

Maya laughed. "That's the whole point of a surprise."

Family members approached us, giving out hugs and wishing her a happy birthday. When everyone had greeted us, Charlye glanced at me. "You really did this?"

Pulling her to me, I kissed her. Once, twice, and a third time on the tip of her nose. "Because you deserve to be celebrated. Today and every day."

She whispered against my mouth. "Wait until we get home."

I groaned. "This is a big house, Pretty. We can disappear easily."

Charlye laughed. "Thank you."

"Brunch is served!" Duke announced. "Char, come here. You get the first waffle."

Justus held up a box. "This came for you today." He handed Charlye the gift.

"What is it?" Charlye examined it, then shook it. "Did it have a return address?" The room descended into silence, but she didn't seem to notice. She opened the card and read aloud. "Because I can't wait to spend the rest of my life with…" She met my gaze. "Dex?"

Behind me, I heard a squeal and figured it was Elise or Bliss. Next to me, my mother and father were riveted to the scene. To my left, Maya had tears in her eyes. Charles handed her a tissue.

"Oh my God," Charlye whispered.

I didn't drop to one knee. I didn't recite a poem. I didn't play a song. That wasn't me. That wasn't us. "Marry me. Because I want to move *slow* with you forever."

Tears streamed from her eyes. "Are you sure?"

I brushed the moisture from her face, placed a kiss on her brow, her nose, her cheeks, and finally her mouth. "Very sure."

She kissed me then. "I'll do everything and nothing with you, Dex. So, wifey me, please." She held out her hand.

I slid the ring on her finger and tugged her to me, kissing her long and hard. As our family celebrated around us, the only person I could see, the only person I could hear, the only person I could feel, was Charlye. "I love you."

"I love you too." She scanned the room and whispered, "Although, next time, can you make my surprise a little more low-key?" She lifted her hand and closed her thumb and forefinger, leaving a tiny space in between. "Just a little." I laughed. "Because this is a bit much."

Elise pulled Charlye away and I stared at my future wife as she embraced my family and hers. I'd once thought our timing was all wrong, but now I believed everything happened the way it was supposed to happen. Our journey, our experiences brought us to where we were now. And I wouldn't change anything. Because I knew that I would always honor her, that I would always chase her, that I would always love her—*for as long as we both shall live.*

Epilogue

YOU BELONG TO ME

Dexter

November, This Year

Charlye moaned. "Dex, you can't…"

I kissed my way down her body. "I'm not ready to let you go yet." I dipped my tongue in her belly button, licked my way down to the apex of her thighs. "And you asked, so I have to deliver."

She giggled. "That was two orgasms ago." She purred, when I slipped one finger, then another, inside her pussy. "Everyone is waiting on us."

"So?" I circled her clit with my tongue before I sucked it into my mouth.

I can do this forever. And I would. Forever with Charlye was a foregone conclusion. As we neared our wedding day, we'd settled into a routine, one that was new and familiar, comfortable and exciting. Our life together was exactly what *she* wanted and what *I* needed. Waking up with her in the mornings and falling asleep with her in the evenings was everything. I couldn't wait to make her Mrs. Young.

It didn't take long for Charlye to come, with my name on her lips. Not done with her yet, we made slow love until we both fell over again.

"I love you," she whispered against my mouth. "So much."

I kissed her. "Love you too."

"I can't wait to be your wife."

I traced the line of her nose. "Three more months." I stared at her in awe. The woman that I'd always wanted, the woman I'd loved for so long was going to be mine. Officially. "So beautiful."

"All yours too," she said.

A smile tugged at my lips, because she always seemed to know what I was thinking. "That's what I like to hear."

A slow smile spread over her full lips. "I'm so sleepy." She bit my neck, then traced the spot with her tongue. "This is your fault."

I chuckled, pulling her against my side. "We could always stay in here." I kissed her forehead. "We don't have to leave our room."

She cuddled against me. "And incur Dallas' wrath? I'll pass on that. Besides, I've never been to Denver. I want to get out and explore."

For the past several years, my siblings and I had spent the weekend after Thanksgiving together. Usually, we rented an Airbnb in a random spot on the map and just chilled with one another. No agenda, just us. It had started when Duke moved out of the state. After his first holiday away, we'd decided to fly out and surprise him because

Bliss managed to convince us that he looked and sounded lonely on FaceTime. Of course, the surprise was on us when we'd barged in on him and one of his *non*-girlfriends who'd flown out to spend Thanksgiving with him. And, of course, that simple fact hadn't deterred Dallas from making this a tradition.

Once my siblings started coupling up, we decided to extend the weekend and include all the significant others. Even with my sister's bossy ways, *Young'uns Weekend* was something I looked forward to every year. This was the first time we'd invited another group to join us. Charlye's siblings had flown in too. And although Elise couldn't come because she'd recently had her baby, Charlye agreed to FaceTime her for all the fun events and pick Secret Santa names for her and Jay.

"Have you heard from Tristan?" Charlye asked.

I thought about that for a moment. In all the years we'd been doing this, my oldest brother had yet to attend. Not that he hadn't been invited, though. I was sure Dallas sent him the details every year. "No. I don't expect to see him."

She flashed a sad smile. "Does that upset you?"

I shrugged. "Not really." My relationship with my oldest brother wasn't the best. Dallas and Paityn were the only two siblings who spoke to him, sometimes. Wasn't for the lack of trying on my part, though. Growing up, he'd been deemed the *fun-killer* of the family. Even so, I'd spent years trying to build something with him to no avail. But I'd always held out hope that we could re-connect one day. Unfortunately, my brother seemed to prefer being on his own. So, I'd learned not to question it. When he was ready to be around us, he would come.

"I just hate that he's not even coming to the wedding."

My brother hadn't RSVP'd or even acknowledged that he even knew I was engaged. "It is what it is," I said.

The smell of bacon and the sound of laughter signaled that everyone was up and ready to get the day started. We stayed there for a few minutes in comfortable silence before Charlye sat up and stretched, not even caring that she wasn't covered. "Shower? I'll let you wash my back."

Several minutes later, we emerged from our suite and joined the rest of our family in the kitchen. But not before I tried to convince Charlye to stay in our personal haven for a little longer.

Paityn and Duke manned the kitchen, barking orders, scrambling eggs, flipping pancakes and stirring grits. Asa and Bishop were on toast duty, Justus and Isis were mixing mimosas, Preston and Lennox were moving furniture to make room, Harper was setting the table, and Dallas and Bliss were huddled in the corner making plans. It was all hands on deck. Well, except for Blake who was drinking coffee and watching everyone else work. Charlye jumped right in, helping Harper with the flatware.

I approached Duke. "Need any help?"

Duke lifted his eyes, glanced at Charlye, then back at me. He smirked. "You can fix Charlye's ponytail. It's wild as fuck."

Charlye's eyes widened signaling she'd overheard him. "Oh shit." She bolted from the room.

Harper threw a muffin at Duke. "Don't do my sister like that, bruh."

Duke pitched it back at him. "*My* sister can get it just like everyone else here."

Justus cracked up and gave Duke a pound. "Thanks for taking that one, man. I was just getting ready to mess with her about that."

"She should know better by now," Duke added. "And

once you taste Paityn's blueberry muffins, Harp, you're going to be pissed you wasted one of them."

Paityn bumped Duke's hip. "Thanks, brother. I know how to do a thing or two in the kitchen."

Duke hugged her. "I taught you well."

She swatted him with her dish towel. "Other way around, Duke."

Blake walked over to the island and swiped a sausage link off the platter. "Y'all talk too much." She patted her belly. "I'm hungry as hell."

Charlye re-entered the kitchen, ponytail fixed. Everyone clapped. And she took a bow.

I pulled her to me and whispered against her ear. "I can mess your hair up again any time. Just say the word."

She laughed. "I would let you, but those pancakes…" She kissed me. "Later, though."

Dallas chimed in, "Nah, girl. We have plans. After we draw names for Secret Santa."

Asa groaned. "It's time to retire Secret Santa, sis."

"Nope." Dallas said. "Never."

After breakfast, we'd piled into the game room of the house. When we booked this house, we made sure there would be room for all of us to gather in one place. The more our family grew, the larger the space we needed.

Blake slid onto a barstool. "Dallas, pass me the pitcher of mimosas. "When is Demi getting here? She's going to be mad she missed the pancakes."

"They're all gone?" Dallas asked.

"Harper and Justus tore them bad boys up," Bliss explained.

Dallas checked her watch and frowned. "Her flight landed an hour ago. She should be here any minute." Dallas's best friend, Demi, had been part of our family since they were young. She'd even lived with us for several years. "I'll call her."

Charlye sat down on my lap. "Remind me to hire Duke to cook breakfast forever." She brushed her lips over mine. "Matter of fact, can he move in with us?"

"Hell nah." Duke shook his head. "No. I'm not doing that shit."

Charlye gaped. "Really? You just told me that you'd help anyway you can."

"You know I was bullshitting, right?" Duke said.

Blake giggled. "He's so stupid."

I steeled my own smile when Charlye looked at me. "What?" I asked.

She narrowed her eyes. "He gets on my nerves."

I laughed then. "Join the club."

"Look who I found." Dallas walked in the room with Demi. "She pulled up right as I was calling her."

Demi greeted everyone with hugs, except for Duke who she greeted with a punch on his shoulder. "That's for not saving me any pancakes."

Blake sipped her drink. "They were slappin' too."

Duke stood. "That's why I'm about to give the short stack I hid for you to Harp's greedy ass."

Demi's face lit up. "You saved me some?" She hugged him and kissed his cheek. "Thank you."

We spent the afternoon playing cards and games, just being together. Charlye and her siblings fit in well with us. Which wasn't surprising since we'd grown up together.

When Dallas announced the Secret Santa drawing, we all turned our attention to her. She sat on Preston's lap and shook the box of names. "We're so thankful that the Burke family decided to join us this year. I imagine this annual event will get bigger and better as we continue to add new people to our family. Y'all know I take this seriously. So don't make me call you to check on your gift progress." She glared at Asa. "If I have to, it's on sight. Remember that."

Asa lifted his hands up. "Why are you singling me out?"

"Because you're always late," Bliss said. "And cheap. Do better, baby brother."

Dallas gave a rundown of the rules again. "Okay, are we ready?"

"Where's Tristan?" Harper asked. "I haven't seen him in a minute. Does he not participate in Secret Santa?"

I caught the way Dallas glanced over at Demi, flashing a sad smile. I wasn't the only one that was paying attention either. Duke was staring at her too. The tick in his jaw let me know he wasn't happy either. Bliss shared a weird look with Paityn, but the two of them just sighed.

Paityn cleared her throat. "He's busy."

Harper shrugged. "Okay."

Blake opened her mouth to speak, but Lennox placed a finger over her mouth and shook his head subtly. She grumbled a curse and folded her arms over her chest.

"What the hell just happened?" Charlye whispered. "This is awkward."

I realized that I'd been so preoccupied with Charlye that I missed something important. "No idea," I muttered. But I definitely planned to ask questions later.

"Dallas, come on," Asa prodded, obviously sensing the calm before the storm. "We're ready."

"Right." Dallas stood. "Let's get this party started."

Everyone had just picked their names from the box when I heard a gasp. Frowning, I looked at Bliss. I followed her startled gaze to the door, where Tristan stood.

My oldest brother entered the room slowly, his eyes

meeting all of ours. "What's up? Am I too late to draw a name?"

Be sure to keep reading for an excerpt from the next Young in Love Book, It's Not Them, It's Only Her (Duke and Demi's story).

Young in Love Series

Her Little Secret (Prelude)
It's Not Me, It's You
It's Not Love, It's Business
It's Not the Hookup, It's the Chase
It's Not Them, It's Only Her
It's Not Forever, It's For Now

Excerpt: It's Not Them, It's Only Her

YOUNG IN LOVE, BOOK FOUR

*T*he first hit didn't faze me. Because that muthafucka was weak. Always had been a punk. I was able to knock his ass out before his brothers joined the fight. I held my own for about ten minutes before I felt the blade slice into my side. Dropping to my knees, I placed pressure over the wound as another assailant knocked the wind out of me with a swift kick to my stomach. When I reached out to grab his ankle, I noticed my hands were covered with blood. My blood. *Shit.*

"Stay the hell away from my wife," the weak muthafucka spat from behind his brother.

I snickered, even as a sharp pain radiated down my leg. "Maybe if you knew how to take care of her, she wouldn't be trying to get in my bed." The right hook to my jaw caught me off guard, but it wasn't delivered by that asshole. Once again, one of his brothers had delivered a devastating blow. "The fact that you can't even fight me yourself tells me all I need to know."

I lunged for him, getting a few punches in before another brother—the one who looked like he spent his days lifting weights—slammed me onto the ground. In my attempt to shield my head from the hard cement, I landed on my hand, causing sharp pain to shoot from my finger to my elbow. *Shit, it's probably fractured.* I groaned, rolling over onto my back. And his big ass laughed. "You just don't learn, do you?" he taunted.

"Fuck you," I growled. "You better hope you kill me, because when I find yo' ass, when I'm not potentially bleeding out, I'm not coming to play."

His answer was a kick to my other side.

After taking several more severe hits, I couldn't find the strength to get up. As I struggled to catch my breath, I wondered if this was it for me. If the brutal beating and blood loss didn't kill me, dehydration and this damn Louisiana heat would. Them dusty-ass niggas probably thought the same because they scurried away like the pussies they were. I forced my eyes open but could only see out of one. The excruciating pain in my side had dulled to a small ache, but it still hurt to breathe. *Probably a broken rib.* Or several.

A moment later, I'd given up on driving myself to the hospital or even walking to my car. Luckily, I couldn't even feel the sweltering hard concrete beneath me anymore. My brief time in medical school made me acutely aware of my precarious situation. Dizziness. Shortness of breath. I was cold. And tired as hell. If I lost consciousness, I could die.

I managed to lift my arm, relieved that my Apple Watch wasn't damaged. Using all my energy, I asked Siri to dial the first name I could think.

She answered on the third ring. "What the hell is wrong with you? Calling this early in the morning."

Under normal circumstances, I would've told her she wasn't doing anything but sleeping anyway. Talking shit was my love language, but I especially loved the banter between *us*. But because I could barely get a word out, I simply muttered, "Come."

My arm fell under the weight of my injuries, and I promised myself I would fuck them muthafuckas up the next time I saw them. It took a damn stab wound and five big-ass niggas to knock me down. *But is this going to take me out?*

As the minutes ticked by, I found myself thinking of my family, of my parents, Always so giving, so understanding. They'd given us a blueprint to live by, taught us how to navigate the world while Black. They'd shown us unconditional love in action every day. Never made me choose between what *they* wanted and what *I* wanted. They'd only encouraged me to go after what made me happy.

My mother once told me to stop taking so many risks, to stop tempting fate. If she only knew the shit I'd done… Aside from this particular situation, I'd fucked up more times than I'd ever admit to her. What would she do if I died in the street alone over some bullshit? I chose to mess around with a married woman and now bore the brunt of her husband's anger. In my defense, she'd told me she was separated. I didn't believe her ass, though. I just didn't care. Maybe because I was young and cocky. More likely because she was fine as hell, and I was a man-whore. At least, according to my sisters and Skye.

In my weakened state, I sent up a silent prayer, going through the Lord's Prayer and asking for forgiveness and protection as my mom and Sister Pearl had taught me back in the day. All those years in Sunday School mattered. A moment after I sealed my prayer with an "Amen," I wondered if God even heard me. It wasn't like I'd spent so much time talking to Him. But I wanted to plead my case, though, to argue that my brothers and sisters needed me. Well, six of them needed me. Not Tristan. He didn't need shit, but I could imagine even he would be devastated if I was no longer here to blame for his shortcomings.

Who's going to tell everyone when they're fucking up? Paityn would blame herself, for not being there, for not giving me enough love and understanding. But she'd always been a person I could count on and the only person that might be able to beat me in the kitchen. *Maybe.* My baby sister, Blake, would probably go to jail or die trying to avenge my death. My chest tightened when I thought of Blake's twin sister, Bliss. All I could see is her sad face in my mind. Dex and Dallas… They called us "The Triples". Dex and I were identical twins and Dallas was our fraternal sister. She always thought that made her an outsider, but she was the best of us. Hell, they all were a hell of a lot better than me. And Asa? My baby brother would probably just leave. He was good at disappearing. Guess he got that from Tristan. Demi would probably be quiet. She wouldn't speak, she wouldn't cry, she wouldn't engage. It was her defense mechanism, but also her most comfortable state. And she would retreat to that space. X, Zara, Skye… They weren't just friends. They were as much my family as my siblings and parents.

Tears filled my eyes. I wanted all of them to be happy, to know how it felt to be in love, to be loved. I hoped someone would pick up a spatula and cook something besides Paityn. Maybe my niece, Raven? I needed my father to know how much I admired him, how he inspired me to be great. And I prayed my mother didn't blame herself for my mistakes.

As my eyes drifted closed, I whispered my love for them to the night air and imagined their faces in the stars. And then everything went black.

"Duke?"

A voice. *Her* voice pulled me back to the present.

"Please," she whispered, emotion in her voice. "Don't do this to me. Don't make me explain this to Dallas. And your parents? Oh God." I felt her forehead against the side of my face. "I'm sorry. I'm so sorry. I shouldn't have left you there. You were drunk, and I knew it wasn't a good idea."

I winced as a needle pierced my skin. Coolness replaced the sting and I realized someone had started an IV. Other sounds registered next. Male voices, spouting vitals. A hand wrapping a blood pressure cuff around my arm and another set of hands applying pressure on my side.

"Stay with me," she pleaded.

It's not your fault. I wanted to tell her this was on me, that she did nothing wrong, but the darkness pulled me back.

Sometime later, I awoke to unfamiliar voices around me, the sound of a blood pressure cuff deflating, and the consistent beep of the heart monitor. Opening my eyes, I scanned the area and realized I was in a hospital room. Two doctors were off to the side, discussing my care with a nurse while another nurse flushed my IV. And Demi was sitting in the chair next to my bed, her eyes on their movements.

"Not your fault," I managed to say finally.

She jerked back, meeting my good eye with a watery gaze. "Thank God." She stood and hugged me. Gingerly.

"I'm sorry," I whispered.

Demi peered up at the ceiling, before leveling her gaze on me again. "You scared the shit out of me. And you're right, it's not my fault. It's yours." Tears fell down her face. I wanted to wipe them away, but I still couldn't move. "I prayed."

"Me, too." I closed my eyes.

Demi flashed a wobbly smile. "You need to pray

harder, because you look like you've been walking through the valley of the shadow of death. Face all fucked up, eye looking like Rocky's after Apollo Creed won the match."

I would've tried to smile, but I knew it would hurt so I murmured, "You're silly."

"Adrian!" she called, mimicking Rocky in the movie.

"Stop," I chuckled. "You're killing me."

The doctors walked over to us and gave me the rundown of my injuries. They'd operated to stop the internal bleeding and started me on intravenous antibiotics to prevent infection. The good news was the knife didn't hit an artery and my ribs were bruised, not broken. *Just like my life.*

When they left the room, Demi brushed a finger over my brow. "Are you in a lot of pain?"

I shook my head. "Not right now. Did you call my family?"

She quirked an eyebrow. "Did you want me to?"

"No."

"That's what I thought." Her chin trembled. "You could've died."

"I didn't."

"But you *could've*," she reiterated. "I'm glad you didn't, though. Get some rest."

LATER, I woke up in a different room. Demi stood by the window staring outside, her arms folded across her chest. She'd changed clothes and pulled her curls back into a smooth bun. *What day is it?*

A nurse entered the room and smiled. "Hi, Mr. Young. I'm Ariana. I'll be the nurse on call today." I nodded at her and glanced at Demi again. "The attending physician will be in to speak with you momentarily. Can I get you anything right now?"

"No," I grumbled.

Another nurse walked in. She looked vaguely familiar, and I assumed she'd taken care of me before. "Hello, Mr. Young. I wanted to stop in before I head out. I'm on vacation the rest of the week, but I wanted to give you my phone number. Call me if you need anything at all." She handed me a business card.

Demi snatched it out of my hand. With her eyes on mine, she told the nurse, "He won't need this." Then, she met the nurse's horrified gaze. "Enjoy your vacation."

"Ma'am, I—" the nurse sputtered.

"Really?" Demi scoffed. "Ariana seems perfectly capable of taking care of Duke."

"She is," the nurse agreed. "She's one of our best."

"Good to know. Is there a reason you felt the need to hand a patient your personal number—" she threw up finger quotes, "—in case he needs you?"

"No, but—"

"You're that desperate that you're giving a strange man your phone number? A strange man that entered the hospital under mysterious circumstances, obviously beaten to a pulp, with another woman. He could be a drug dealer or a murderer. He could be *my* man and you're, what... flirting with him? Does he look like he's going to call you anytime soon? Because from where I'm standing, he looks pretty fucked up to me."

"But," the young nurse said. "I—"

"Is it protocol to pass your number to patients?" Demi continued relentlessly, her skill in the courtroom shining through with her interrogation of the poor nurse. "Do all patients receive the same level of care at this hospital that you would be on call, even during your vacation, to serve him? Or is it just the fine ones? Maybe I need to verify the rules with your supervisor?"

The nurse stuttered an apology—or fifty—before scurrying out of the room. Demi turned her attention to Ariana and smiled brightly. "Thanks for bringing me breakfast this morning. I appreciate you."

Ariana grinned. "You're welcome. And thank you," she whispered.

I looked back and forth between the two women and realized I'd missed something important. Context. A few minutes later, Ariana was gone, and Demi was back in front of the window.

"You told her," I mumbled, wincing as I shifted to face her. "Ma'am."

"Seriously? She tried it. She's probably older than me." Demi rolled her eyes hard. "Calling me ma'am, like I'm someone's mother."

"And we're not in court, counselor."

"It doesn't matter. The last thing you should be doing is hooking up with anyone else in this city."

"I take it Ariana was in on this takedown."

Demi shrugged, finally turning to me. "She mentioned being harassed by the mean-girl group of nurses led by that heffa who couldn't even start your IV yesterday."

I chuckled. "Alright, then. You did the right thing."

She sat on the edge of the bed, her forehead creased with worry. "Duke, you could've been killed."

"But I wasn't," I reminded her. I focused on her, relieved that I could now see her with both eyes, although the one was still swollen. "We've been over this already. Stop worrying."

"Easy for you to say. You didn't find *me* passed out in some alley, in a pool of blood."

"You already told me off yesterday. What happened?"

"*You* happened," she snapped. "I've thought of nothing else since I saw them wheel your ass into the back of an ambulance. I couldn't sleep, I couldn't eat. I had no idea what I would tell the family if you didn't make it. The initial shock of seeing you like that and the relief I felt when you opened your damn eye has worn off. I'm pissed now. You better be glad I was only a block away. All of this for some woman?" She stood and paced the small room. "I knew something wasn't right about this trip. But, once again, I let you lead me astray." Demi went on and on about warnings, fucking around, and finding out. "I don't blame you, though. This is all on me."

"Right." I'd been around Demi long enough to know that her ire was directed at me because I was there. And she was scared. The real target of her anger wasn't around to feel her wrath. "Did you do what you came here to do?"

She sighed and sat on the edge of the bed. "He stood me up. Again."

"Are you finally ready to let him go?"

The question hung in the air for a moment. It was no secret that Demi had a thing for my brother Tristan. Everyone knew it, including him. As far as I was concerned, he'd led her on, made her think there could be something between them, made her hope that one day they'd be at the same place in life and ready for forever. And she'd let him, through college, law school, and even now that she'd made a name for herself in her career as a divorce attorney. He'd leave. Come back. She'd accept him back in her life and heart, then he'd pull away. Then, the cycle would start over again. Wash. Rinse. Repeat.

Demi averted her gaze, fiddling with the strap of her purse. "Enough about me. This is about you."

"I keep telling you it's never going to work." Most likely

ELLE WRIGHT

because Tristan was an asshole on his best days. And Demi deserved better, but *she* hadn't learned that lesson yet.

She looked at me finally, then changed the subject. "Why would you sleep with that woman knowing she was married? You told me those days were behind you."

I told myself that it was my injuries and not the disappointment written on her face that made my chest tighten. The truth of my past wasn't pretty. I'd had several affairs with unavailable women, mostly because it worked for my lifestyle. No labels. No commitment. No expectations. But I'd vowed to be better in recent years. Not because I had a sudden epiphany about love and marriage, but because I realized I had too much to lose. *Family. Career.* I had many regrets, but dropping out of medical school to pursue culinary art wasn't one of them. I excelled in front of the stove. Food was my safe place. Cooking was my passion. The kitchen was my office.

"I didn't know she was married," I admitted.

Her green eyes flashed to mine. She bit down on her bottom lip. "Really?"

"Do I lie?"

Demi's shoulders sagged. "Never to me," she said. "When did you find out?"

"Tonight. I broke it off, and she called her husband."

"Bitch," she muttered.

"It's over."

Demi met my eyes. "No revenge." When I didn't answer, she squeezed my hand. "Duke? Please, don't go looking for him. Think about the plans you have for your life."

In the past, I wouldn't have thought twice about finding that punk and beating the shit out of him. But Demi was right. I'd come too far to fuck my life up. Maybe

I wouldn't get to him, but I knew people. "I won't," I assured her.

"And no calling someone else to do it either," she said sternly.

I closed my eyes and burrowed into the pillow. "Fine."

I felt her hand on my chest and rested mine on top of hers. "Good. Now, get some rest." Demi walked to the door and peered back at me. "I'll be back in about an hour."

"If I can't go after him, you damn sure better not go see her."

"Shit," Demi hissed, stomping over to the chair next to the bed. "I was just going to have a little talk with her."

A smile tugged at my lips. "A talk with your fists?"

She crossed her arms over her chest and glared at me. "It's alright."

"And you can't tell Blake."

"Damn," she mumbled. "Anyway, we're out of here as soon as the doctor releases you. Go to sleep."

"Whatever you say." It didn't take long to drift off because I knew I was in good hands. That meant more to me than Demi could ever know.

Recommended Reading

Want more of the Youngs?

Blake Young appeared as Ryleigh's friend in my Once Upon a Baby novella, BEYOND EVER AFTER.

Duke Young burst onto the scene in my Pure Talent novels, THE WAY YOU TEMPT ME and THE WAY YOU HOLD ME. And he stole the show.

Dallas Young made her presence known in my Once Upon a Funeral novella, FINDING COOPER.

Duke and Bliss also made an appearance in my novella, SOME KIND OF LOVE.

Meet their extended family in TEN CHRISTMAS SHOTS, which is a follow-up of my first historical romance set in the 1980s, MADE TO HOLD YOU.

Also, did you know that there was another set of Youngs? Yes, you heard that right. Aunt Vicki married someone with her same last name.

I introduced that side of the family in SMOKE IN LOVE, THE SECRETS WE HATE, and THE SECRETS WE CREATE - KNOX.

Please Note: Several of these stories take place around the same time. Some events may happen in multiple books from a different POV.

www.ellewright.com

Acknowledgments

God is able! I'm so thankful.

To my hubby, Jason, you're my forever love. Thanks for supporting me through everything.

To Sherelle and Sheryl… This book wouldn't be what it is without your invaluable advice and unwavering support. Thank you so much for everything!

Midnight, you are the bomb! You already know… Thank you!

A special shout-out to the awesome readers , bloggers, and writers that I've met on this journey. Thanks for your support. I appreciate you!

Connect with Elle!

Thank you for reading Dexter and Char's story! I love to hear from my readers. If you enjoyed *It's Not the Hookup, It's the Chase*, please consider posting a review or sending an email. They really do help. Don't forget to tell your friends!

Subscribe to my Newsletter
New Releases, Upcoming projects, and Freebies!

On Facebook,
Join my cocktail lounge for exclusive updates, drink recipes, and lots of fun!
bit.ly/EllesCocktailLounge

Visit my website: www.ellewright.com

Email me at info@ellewright.com

facebook.com/ellewrightauthor

instagram.com/lwrightauthor

amazon.com/Elle-Wright/e/B00VMEWB78

bookbub.com/profile/elle-wright

Touched By You

Enticed By You

Pleasured By You

Pure Talent Series

(Sexy + Steamy moments + High-powered executives + Drama)

The Way You Tempt Me

The Way You Hold Me

The Way You Love Me

Once Upon a Series

Beyond Forever (Once Upon a Bridesmaid)

Beyond Ever After (Once Upon a Baby)

Finding Cooper (Once Upon a Funeral)

The Secrets We Hate (Once Upon a Murder)

The Secrets We Create - Knox (Once Upon a Murder)

Standalones

The Closing Bid

Irresistible Temptation

The Baes

One More Drink

Ten Christmas Shots

Mr. Down for Whatever

Smoke in Love

Historical Romance

Made To Hold You (The 80s)

Suspense/Thriller

Basement Level 5: Never Scared

About the Author

There was never a time when Elle Wright wasn't about to start a book, wasn't already deep in a book—or had just finished one. She grew up believing in the importance of reading, and became a lover of all things romance when her mother gave her her first romance novel. She lives in Michigan.

Connect with Elle!
www.ellewright.com
info@ellewright.com

www.ingramcontent.com/pod-product-compliance
Lightning Source LLC
Chambersburg PA
CBHW020630250626
47154CB00008B/2621